BUDDHIST TALES for YOUNG and OLD

Volume 4

Stories of the Enlightenment Being

Jātakas 151–200

BUDDHIST TALES for YOUNG and OLD

Volume 4

Stories of the Enlightenment Being

Jātakas 151–200

Interpreted by

KURUNEGODA PIYATISSA MAHA THERA

Stories Retold by

STEPHAN HILLYER LEVITT

Pariyatti Press

Buddhist Tales for Young and Old

Volume 1: STORIES OF THE ENLIGHTENMENT BEING, Jātakas 1–50.
Interpreted by Kurunegoda Piyatissa Maha Thera. Stories Told by Todd Anderson. Illustrated by Sally Bienemann, Millie Byrum, Mark Gilson. 2nd edition, revised and enlarged by Kurunegoda Piyatissa Maha Thera and Stephan Hillyer Levitt. Parkside Hills, New York: Buddhist Literature Society, Inc., 2013. (1st edition, under the title PRINCE GOODSPEAKER, STORIES 1–50, 1995.)

Volume 2: STORIES OF THE ENLIGHTENMENT BEING, Jātakas 51–100, 514.
Interpreted by Kurunegoda Piyatissa Maha Thera. Stories Told by Todd Anderson. Illustrated by John Patterson. 2nd edition, revised and enlarged by Kurunegoda Piyatissa Maha Thera and Stephan Hillyer Levitt. Parkside Hills, New York: Buddhist Literature Society, Inc., 2013. (1st edition, under the title KING FRUITFUL, STORIES 51–100, 1996. 2nd ptg. of the 1st edition, together with KING SIX TUSKER AND THE QUEEN WHO HATED HIM, CHADDANTA-JATAKA (NO. 514) appended, [2004].)

Volume 3: STORIES OF THE ENLIGHTENMENT BEING, Jātakas 101–150.
Interpreted by Kurunegoda Piyatissa Maha Thera. Stories Retold by Stephan Hillyer Levitt. Parkside Hills, New York: Buddhist Literature Society, Inc., 2007.

Volume 4: STORIES OF THE ENLIGHTENMENT BEING, Jātakas 151–200.
Interpreted by Kurunegoda Piyatissa Maha Thera. Stories Retold by Stephan Hillyer Levitt. Parkside Hills, New York: Buddhist Literature Society, Inc., 2009.

Volume 5: STORIES OF THE ENLIGHTENMENT BEING, Jātakas 201–250.
Interpreted by Kurunegoda Piyatissa Maha Thera. Stories Retold by Stephan Hillyer Levitt. Parkside Hills, New York: Buddhist Literature Society, Inc., 2012.

Relief from Ajantā of Queen Subhaddā of 'The Story of the Elephant with Six Tusks' (*Chaddanta-Jātaka*, Jātaka No. 514)

Pariyatti Press
an imprint of
Pariyatti Publishing
www.pariyatti.org

First Pariyatti Edition, 2024
Published with the consent of Buddhist Literature Society, Inc.

ISBN: 978-1-68172-660-1 (Print)
ISBN: 978-1-68172-684-7 (PDF)
ISBN: 978-1-68172-685-4 (ePub)
ISBN: 978-1-68172-686-1 (Mobi)
Library of Congress Control Number: 2024936371

Cover illustration by Sally Bienemann, assisted by Arlene Yellen and cover design by Nalin Ariyarathne.

Foreword

This volume continues the translation of the Jātaka stories begun earlier.

The reader response received for the previous three volumes has encouraged us to persist with this work for our readers' benefit. We thank our readers. And we thank our publishers, the Buddha Educational Foundation of Taiwan, R.O.C. for their contribution to the world by their giving of Dhamma during the last few decades. They have done a marvelous service by their Dhamma-Dāna.

We were happy to see several printings of the previous volumes issued by them for the benefit of the public. We thank them for their untiring service and their financial output towards this exercise. This takes us back to the words of the Buddha, "The gift of Dhamma excels all others [*sabbadānam dhammadānam jināti*]".

We expect to present the Jātaka stories in batches of fifty stories in each volume. But toward the end of the Jātaka-s, as the stories happen to stretch longer, this will have to be adjusted accordingly. We plan to publish in the future all the stories in simple English.

In Sri Lankan history it is found that Sri Lankan Buddhist culture developed mostly by what came down through word of mouth and by the hearing and reading of the Jātaka stories and the Sutta-s. People paid attention to what they learnt through these stories, just as they paid attention to their Sutta studies.

In keeping with this, in this volume, as the stories lend themselves to it, we have included in the footnotes more information of general interest that explains allusions and passing references in the stories. We hope the reader will find these footnotes useful, and that they will not distract from the flow of the stories.

The sources used in the preparation of this translation are as follows:

1. *Jātakapāli, with the Sinhala Translation*, by Ven. Madihe Siri Paññasīha Mahā Nāyaka Thera, 3 vols. *Buddha Jayanti Tripitaka Series*, vols. 30–32. Colombo: Published under the patronage of Democratic Socialist Republican Government of Sri Lanka, 1983-86. Original Pāli Jātaka stories with the Pāli commentary, in Sinhala script with a modern Sinhala translation.
2. *Bhadantācariya Buddhaghosa Mahā Thera's Commentary to the Jātaka Pāli*, rev. and ed. by Ven. Pandit Widurupola Piyatissa Mahā Nāyaka Thera, 7 vols. *Simon Hewavitarne Bequest*, vols. 20, 24, 32, 36, 37, 39, 41. Colombo: Published by the Trustees, 1926-39. Commentary in Pāli on the Pāli Jātaka stories, based on older sources, attributed to the 5th c. C.E. scholar Buddhaghosa. An earlier edition in Sinhala script of the Pāli text in 1. above.
3. *Panṣiyapaṇas Jātaka Pota*, by Virasiṃha Pratirāja. Ed. D. Jinaratana. 1927; 5th ptg. Colombo: Jinalankara Press, 1928 A late 13th – early 14th c. C.E. translation of the Pāli Jātaka stories into Sinhala by a minister of Kings Parākramabāhu II, III, and IV.
4. *Pansiyapaṇas Jātaka Pota*, by Virasiṃha Pratirāja. Ed. Vēragoḍa Amaramōli. Colombo: Ratnakara Bookshop, 1961. A different edition of 3. above.
5. *Pansiyapaṇas Jātaka Pot Vahansē*, by H. W. Nimal Prematilake. 1963; Rpt. Bandaragama: H. W. Nimal Prematilaka, 1987. Recent Sinhala summaries of the Pāli Jātaka stories.
6. *The Jātaka, or Stores of the Buddha's Former Births*, 6 vols., index. Ed. E. B. Cowell. 1895–1913; Rpt. London: Pali Text Society, 1981. English translation of the Pāli Jātaka stories done by various hands. Contains the stories of the present, which are from the commentary.
7. *Ummagga Jataka (The Story of the Tunnel)*, translated from the Sinhalese by David Karunaratne. Colombo: M. D. Gunasena and Co., Ltd., 1962. Modern English translation of the *Mahā-Ummagga-Jātaka* [No. 546].

The numbers of the various Jātaka stories in this translation are as in 1. and 6. above. The sequence is also the same as in 2., but the numbering in that is different. 2. numbers the Jātaka stories according to book, chapter, and Jātaka story within a chapter.

We wish to share the merit accrued by us through the translation effort involved here with everyone who has partaken of this work.

May all be well and happy!

Kurunegoda Piyatissa Nayaka Maha Thero
Stephan Hillyer Levitt, Ph.D.
May, 2008

Buddhist Literature Society, Inc.
New York Buddhist Vihara
214-22 Spencer Avenue
Parkside Hills, New York 11427-1821, U. S. A.

A Guide to the Pronunciation of Pāli Words and Names

Vowels

a	as *u* in but	u	as *u* in pull	ā	as *a* in father
ū	as *u* in rule	i	as *i* in pin	e	as *ay* in say
ī	as *i* in machine	o	as *o* in go		

Consonants and Nasals

k (guttural) like the English *k* in take or pick. kh as *kh* in lakehouse. g as *g* in pig. gh as *gh* in doghouse. The nasal ṅ is used with k, kh, g, and gh.

c (palatal) similar to *ch* in chalk, but unaspirated. ch as *ch* in chalk or church.

j like the English *g* in page. jh as *j* in joy, but even more aspirated. The nasal ñ as in Spanish Español is used with c, ch, j, and jh.

ṭ a retroflex sound, pronounced with the tongue curled back so that it touches the roof of the mouth. ṭh is the same sound, but aspirated. ḍ and ḍh are the voiced counterparts of these sounds. ṇ is the retroflex nasal. The difference between these sounds and the dentals, without dots, is not important for the general reader.

t (dental) similar to *t* in French or Italian. th as *th* in anthill. d similar to *d* in pod or paid. dh as *dh* in roundhouse. The nasal n is used with t, th, d, and dh.

p (labial) as *p* in English up. ph as *ph* in uphill. b as *b* in rub. bh as *bh* in clubhouse. The nasal m is used with p, ph, b, and bh.

ṁ as *ng* in sing. This is a nasal sound that lacks the closure of the organs required for the other nasal sounds.

Semivowels

y, r, l, v similar to their English counterparts. ḷ is a retroflex variant of l.

Sibilant

s as *s* in saint or hiss.

Aspirate

h as *h* in hit.

Contents

151

The Story of Advice to a King
(*Rājovāda-Jātaka*)

When the Buddha was living in the monastery in Jeta Grove, this Jātaka story was delivered as advice to a king. The present story here is similar to the present story of the *Tesakuṇa-Jātaka* [No. 521].

[One day King Pasenadi of Kosala went to see the Buddha to discuss the Dhamma (the law). Buddha said, "A righteous king must rule his country by the tenfold laws for righteous ruling by a king (*dasarājadhamma*)."[1] The Buddha admonished him to be righteous in ruling. "If a king is righteous in ruling, his officials also will be righteous. If a king is not righteous, his officials also will not be righteous. In ancient times, even when there was no Buddha's teaching, wise kings ruled their countries by following wise people. By doing so, they went to heaven." Then the king asked, "Your reverence, how was it?" And the Buddha explained the tenfold laws for the righteous ruling of a country, and disclosed how it was.]

Here, King Pasenadi of Kosala, because he was judging a difficult case, could not go to visit the Buddha in the morning as usual.[2] After taking his lunch, he washed his fingers. Even before drying his fingers, he got on his chariot and went to see the Buddha. He knelt down before the presence of the Buddha, and sat on the side.

Buddha, addressing the king, said, "Your lordship, why did you come here this afternoon, after not having come in the morning?" The

---

1 These tenfold laws for a righteous king are generosity [*dāna*], morality [*sīla*], liberality [*pariccāga*], uprightness [*ajjava*], gentleness [*maddava*], self-control [*tapo*], lack of anger [*akkodha*], absence of cruelty [*avihiṁsā*], patience [*khanti*], and being moderate [*avirodhana*].

2 King Pasenadi of Kosala was in the habit of visiting the Buddha three times a day, morning, noon, and evening.

king said, "Revered one, I had a difficult case to judge that had to do with morality. For this reason, I could not come in the morning." The Buddha said, "Now, as king, you can judge such cases in a righteous way since you have a Buddha such as me as a guide. But in ancient times, even those who judged such cases without such a one's guidance, were able to do so without being partial on account of greed, hatred, fear, and ignorance." Then the king invited the Buddha to disclose the story of the olden time.

Buddha said thus:

At one time, the city of Benares was ruled by King Brahmadatta. At that time the Enlightenment Being was conceived in the womb of his crown queen, and was delivered after nine-and-a-half months.

On his naming day, they named him Prince Brahmadatta. When he grew up, he was sent to the foremost teacher at that time, and was educated and trained in all arts. After returning to Benares, he became the king of the city when his father died. He ruled the country without being partial to anyone. He ruled in a righteous and pleasing manner, and there was no objection from anyone regarding his rule. Among his subjects, there was no conflict. Because of this, the courts became empty. Ministers spent the day without any cases to decide. In the evening they went home without having done anything. As there were no people coming to have their complaints judged, the ministers just wasted their time.

The days went on this way without the trying of any wrong deeds in the country. The king thought, "My country is in peace and happiness. Nevertheless, I would like to examine myself. Is there anybody in the country who might accuse me of a fault?" Thinking so, every night he went into the city and listened to what people were saying about him. He did not find anyone who mentioned his having any fault. People said, "May our righteous king live a long, happy life!" He never heard from anybody that he had done a wrong deed. So he thought, "As I am living in the city, people may not be willing to say any of my faults out of fear. I will go to villages." Making such a decision, he disguised himself and went to remote villages. He went from home to home, but still he did not hear anyone saying that he had any fault. Finally he decided, "No doubt these people do not say anything against me because they are afraid of me." Thinking so, he decided to go even further into the countryside in remote areas of the kingdom.

He then handed over the kingdom to his ministers to rule. With only his chariot, he went to the remote countryside. There, also, he found no one saying anything bad about him. Finally, he decided to return to Benares.

On his way, he met on the road King Mallika of the city of Sāvatthi. He also was examining whether there were people who would speak of him any fault. He as well did not hear anyone saying anything bad about him.

[The two charioteers argued over who should pass first.] The king of Sāvatthi's charioteer, thinking that he would say his king's good qualities, said, however, only bad things about him. He said, "Our king always does bad deeds to bad people, and he does good deeds to good people. To liars, our king also lies, and he wins. To those who speak truthfully, he speaks the same way. To miserly people, he also is miserly. To generous people, he is generous. These are the good qualities of our king. Therefore, you should honor our king and move to the side so we can pass."

Listening to him, the charioteer of the king of Benares said, "You said of your king only bad qualities, thinking that you were saying good qualities. Listen to our king's good qualities. Our king wins the minds of angry people without showing anger. He wins over misers through generosity. He wins over liars through truthfulness. These are the good qualities of our king. Therefore, give us the way."[3]

King Mallika who was inside his chariot, hearing these words, got out of his chariot, unyoked the bulls from his chariot, and by hand moved his chariot to the side of the road. He then requested the king of Benares to pass with his chariot. The king of Benares said to King Mallika of Sāvatthi, "You are a good king. Go and rule your country as I rule mine with virtuousness and righteousness." Admonishing him in this way, the

3 Compare *Dhammapada*, verse 223.

king of Benares passed first and went to his city. In the course of time, he passed away.

"The Venerable Moggallāna was at that time King Mallika's charioteer. The Venerable Ānanda was King Mallika. The Venerable Sāriputta was the charioteer of the king of Benares. And I was the one born as the king of Benares."

Saying so, the Buddha ended the Jātaka story of advice to a king.

The moral: "One will always win by doing good."

152

The Story of a Jackal
(*Sigāla-Jātaka*)

When the Buddha was residing at the gabled palace in the city of Vesāli, there was a certain barber in that city who was always going to the king's palace. He was the hairdresser for the various queens and princesses, and the barber for the men of the royal family. He was as faithful to the royal family as he was to the Buddha, the Dhamma [the law], and the Saṅgha [the community of monks]. He diligently followed the five precepts,[4] and he used to go see the Buddha every day.

One day, the hairdresser took one of his sons to the royal palace. At that time, a princess came by. She was so irresistibly beautiful that on seeing her, the hairdresser's son became infatuated with her. With such desires, he returned home and lay on his bed without eating or drinking. The hairdresser said, "Don't you know that you were born in a family unsuitable for her, being a barber's son. She was born in a royal family by both her father and her mother. Such a virgin will never marry you. Therefore, do not grieve. I will bring you a beautiful maiden from a barber's family in the future. Do not grieve." The son did not pay attention to his father's words. After that, other relatives, even younger sisters, and relatives of in-laws and trustworthy friends, all advised him, but he did not listen. He became dehydrated, and he died out of grief from not eating or drinking.

The father arranged his funeral, and after cremating him, did all rites necessary to be done for a departed son.

---

4 The five precepts are not to kill, not to steal, not to commit adultery, not to lie, and not to intoxicate the mind.

Because of all this, the father could not go to visit the Buddha. When he had finished the period of mourning, he took flowers, incense, and lights, and he went to see the Buddha. When he saw the Buddha, Buddha asked him, "Oh devout layman, what is the reason for your not coming for so long?" The barber said, "Revered sir, my son became infatuated with a certain princess of the royal family, and he being unable to give up his infatuation, died by starving. Because of that, I was unable to come to visit you." On hearing this news, the Buddha said, "Oh devout layman, not only did he die in this life from infatuation with a noble person, but also in the past he died in this way."

Invited by the barber, the Buddha disclosed this hidden story of a jackal:

At one time, when King Brahmadatta was ruling in Benares, the Enlightenment Being was born as a lion in the forest. He had six younger brother lions. A seventh sibling, who was the youngest, was a lioness. They all lived together in a certain golden cave. Nearby, on a silver rock in a crystal cave, there lived a jackal.

After a time, the Enlightenment Being's parents died. Since then, the Enlightenment Being and his six brothers would leave their sister in the golden cave, and go to hunt for meat. After killing an animal, they would eat at that same spot, and then bring some meat for their sister. In this way, time passed.

The jackal who lived on the silver rock thought, "This young lioness has no parents any more. The brothers go out to hunt for meat every day. Why should I not go and try to seduce the lioness, so that I might live with her?" Thinking so, he came down from the silver rock to the golden cave and talked to the lioness. "Look, you have four feet, and I also have four feet. So, why should we not become mates? If you would be my wife, I would be your husband." He uttered such words in a seductive fashion.

Listening to his words, the lioness thought, "This one was born as a menial four-footed animal. I was born as a noble four-footed animal. How can there be trust between us?" She thought further, "Hearing such lusty words from a jackal, I ought to kill him by biting his neck. I should not kill him, though, until after telling my brothers when they come back."

At the same time, one lion from among the seven brothers returned with meat. He carried the meat to her, put it before her, and said, "Younger sister, eat this meat." The lioness did not eat. She was sad. The lion asked, "What is the reason for your unhappiness?" She told him what had happened. He got angry, and asked, "Where is that jackal?" She said, "Look there. He is on the silver rock, [lying in the sky]." Hearing her words, the lion got very angry and jumped up toward the crystal cave at the top of the silver rock. He hit his chest on the crystal cave, and fell down and died. Six of the brothers died in this way.

The Enlightenment Being returned seventh. On hearing the news from his lioness sister, he thought, "There is no such thing as a jackal lying in the sky. He must be in a crystal cave." Thinking so, he determined the path by which the jackal would come down when he wanted to eat meat, and [placing himself at its foot] he roared a roar that sounded as if the earth were cracking during a thunderstorm. On hearing that roaring noise the jackal became very afraid, and his heart burst and he died.

Buddha continued:

Because of the lioness, the jackal died from fear of the lion's roar. After killing that jackal, the lion returned to the golden cave and found out that his brothers were dead. The lion comforted his sister, who was grieving. After that, they lived in a righteous way and died according to their Kamma [actions].

"The jackal at that time was this hairdresser's son. The lioness was the Licchavi princess. The six lion brothers are now six monks. And I who am now the wholly enlightened being was born at that time as the oldest lion brother."

In this way, the Buddha ended 'The Story of a Jackal'.

The moral: "Foolish thoughts bring disaster."

153

The Story of a Boar
(*Sūkara-Jātaka*)

At one time, when the fully enlightened one was living at Jetavanārāma, he advised the monks from the doorstep of his scented chamber [and he retired].

Venerable Sāriputta and Moggallāna, kneeling down and respecting the Buddha, each went to his own chamber. Then the Venerable Moggallāna, who had retired for only a short time, decided to go to the Venerable Sāriputta who was together with some disciples in his room. He asked some questions.

Venerable Sāriputta was at his preaching pulpit fanning himself. He answered all the questions asked by the Venerable Moggallāna with such detail, it was as if he was displaying in his hand the light from the rising moon. This asking of questions by the Venerable Moggallāna, and their being answered by the Venerable Sāriputta, was witnessed by many monks, nuns, laymen, and laywomen, who were all very interested. They listened intently to the explanations of the Dhamma [the teaching of the Buddha].

At that time, one old monk thought, "Right now, it would be good for me to ask a question also. If Venerable Sāriputta fails to answer, people will respect me a lot, thinking that he is one who does not understand the discipline, and that I am a wise monk." And he approached Venerable Sāriputta and said, "Venerable Sāriputta, I also would like to ask a question. Do I have permission?" He then said gibberish.

On hearing this, Venerable Sāriputta thought, "This old monk said whatever came to his mouth, without any meaning. How can I waste my time by responding?" Placing his fan on the table in front of him, he went into his room. Venerable Moggallāna also went to his room.

The laymen and laywomen thought that they were now missing the interesting Dhamma discussion of those two monks because of this old monk. And they chased after him to attack him. He ran with fear, and [in the night] fell into an old cesspool and became loathsome, being smeared over with filth. On seeing this, the laymen and laywomen went to see the Buddha in the middle of the night.

The Buddha asked, "Why are you lay people coming at this improper time?" On hearing the news, he said, "Not only at this time, but even in the past, this monk has been smeared with filth by comparing himself with noble ones." The lay people asked the Buddha to disclose the story to them. And the Buddha told them the story of former times:

At one time, when King Brahmadatta was ruling in Benares, the Enlightenment Being was born as a king of lions.

At that time, there was a herd of boars nearby a certain lake that scavenged for food in its vicinity. The Enlightenment Being, who had been born as a lion, used to take his food in that same area.

Once, after the Enlightenment Being had eaten food with the other lions, he came to that lake to drink water. At the same time, a large boar after having his meal also came down to the lake to drink water. When the Enlightenment Being saw the boar, he thought, "If this boar sees me, there is no doubt that he will not come back again to this lake. And then I will not be able to kill him and eat him some other day." Thinking so, he decided not to show himself to the boar, and slipped off in the water coming up at a different location. However, the boar saw him going away in this manner and thought that the lion was going away like that because he was afraid of him. Thinking so, he said out loud to the lion, "Hey, friend! Why are you slinking away like that? I have four feet and you have four feet. So why do you avoid me like that? Come to me and let us fight."

Hearing this challenge of the boar, the lion said, "I can't today. Come a week from today, and we can fight then." Saying so, he went away.

The boar went back to his relatives and told them the news about his impending fight with the lion. The other boars censured him. "Without knowing the strength of the lion, you have picked a fight with him. By this action, you will bring calamity to all of us." The boar then became very afraid. He said to the other boars, "Please, tell me a stratagem by which I can escape from this situation." The other boars said, "If this is so, go to the place nearby where ascetics defecate, and apply their excreta to your body and let it dry every day for the whole seven days of the week. When you go to fight the lion, stay upwind. On smelling the stink of your body, the lion will run away without fighting you." The boar then did as they had advised him, and when he went to fight the lion, he stayed upwind. When the lion came and smelled the boar, he said, "The way that you have come now is a very good trick. If it were not for this, I would have killed you. Right now, I cannot touch you by hand, foot, or mouth.[5] Therefore, you have won." And the lion fled. The boar went back to his relatives and told them that he had won the battle. They rejoiced. But they thought, "The lion will be angry with us. Therefore, it is not good to stay here." And they went away.

"The boar at that time was this monk. The lion was I who have become the Buddha at this time."

Saying so, the Buddha ended 'The Story of a Boar'.

The moral: "If a low status person tries to take on the airs of a noble one, he will show his menial nature nevertheless."

5 In South Asian cultures, the front feet of animals are referred to as their hands. This is especially so for cats, lions, dogs, and other meat eating animals.

154

The Story of a Snake
(*Uraga-Jātaka*)

When the Buddha was living in the Jetavanārāma, there were two soldiers of the king of Kosala who were always angry with each other. The king knew this and advised them not to be angry with one another, but they could not control their anger. The Buddha heard this and one day, while focusing on them out of his compassion, he attained to the mental state of great loving kindness [*mahākaruṇā-samāpatti*] and saw that these two were ready to enter the stream entrance state of mind [*sotāpatti*]. Knowing this, the Buddha went to the home of one of them early in the morning for breakfast. Taking the alms bowl of the Buddha, the soldier invited the Buddha into his home, gave the Buddha a place to sit, and fed the Buddha with gruel and sweets. After eating, Buddha preached to him the value of loving kindness. On hearing that, he attained the stream entrance state of mind. After that, Buddha asked him to carry his alms bowl, and at lunchtime the Buddha went to the other soldier's home with him. The other soldier took the Buddha's alms bowl from his enemy's hands, and fed the Buddha with delicious food and drinks. After he had eaten, the Buddha preached to him as well the value of loving kindness, and he also attained the stream entrance state of mind.

Those two persons could not be reconciled by anyone before, but the Buddha did it. They no longer had any anger toward one another.

The monks who assembled in the preaching hall in the evening of that day said, "Oh friends, those two soldiers who were always angry with one another could not be reconciled by anyone. But the enlightened one united them and tamed them, subduing their anger. This is a great thing." Then the Buddha entered the preaching hall and said, "Oh monks, what were you talking about before I came here?" The monks told the Buddha about what they were talking. And the Buddha said, "It is not only today. Even in ancient times, I have reconciled them." And the monks requested the Buddha to disclose the story of the past. The Buddha started to disclose the story. It was thus:

At one time while King Brahmadatta was ruling Benares, the Enlightenment Being was practicing asceticism in a temple nearby a river.

At that time, there was a great festival in Benares. There came to see the festival a divine snake and a Garuḷa,[6] both disguised as human beings. At the end of the festival, the Garuḷa saw the snake and chased after him. The snake forgot his disguise, assumed his natural snake form, and slithered away rapidly. The ascetic, at that moment, had left aside his saffron cloth on the ground and wearing only a loincloth, had gotten into the river to bathe. Meanwhile, the snake saw the robe and thought, "If I can get underneath the saffron robe, I can save my life." Thinking so, he got underneath the robe. The Garuḷa, who was chasing after him, saw the snake get under the robe. But showing compassion toward the ascetic, he picked up the robe with the snake in it, took it to the ascetic, and said, "Your Venerable sir, I was very hungry and was chasing after a snake. As I am showing compassion and loving kindness toward you, I did not devour the snake that has hidden in your robe. Therefore, please take this robe and give me the snake." The Enlightenment Being, on hearing these words, said, "Garuḷa, it is a very good act that you have done. The divine beings will extend your lifespan. You will obtain the nectar of immortality drunk by divine beings." Blessing him so, the Enlightenment Being came out of the water. And while holding the snake in one hand, he put on his robe. Together with both the Garuḷa and the snake, he went to his temple. There, he preached to both of them the disadvantages of anger. They both, then, became reconciled to one another. Both, who were natural enemies of one another from birth, became reconciled with one another. The Enlightenment Being further advised them both not

6 A Garuḷa is a mythical bird that is a mortal enemy of snakes.

to be antagonistic toward their births. Upon their promising so, he sent them away.

After relating this story, the Buddha said, "The Garuḷa and snake of that time are these two soldiers today. The ascetic was I who have now become the enlightened one." Saying so, he ended this Jātaka story of *Uraga* [a snake].

The moral: "Anger is common. Friendliness is noble."

155

The Story of Gagga

(*Gagga-Jātaka*)

When Buddha was living in Jetavanārāma, one day he came to preach at Rājakārāma temple that had been built and donated by King Pasenadi of Kosala. While he was preaching in the presence of the fourfold followers,[7] the Buddha sneezed. Many monks said, "Blessings upon the Buddha! May the Buddha live long!" Since many monks were blessing the Buddha in this way, it took a long time. Because of this, the delivery of the Dhamma sermon was spoiled.

When this happened, the noble one asked the monks, "Oh monks, by so blessing are you able to increase someone's lifespan? When you do not so bless someone, does it shorten their lifespan?" Then the monks answered, "Honorable sir, such things do not happen." The Buddha said, "Oh monks, if such things do not happen, then from today on even if someone blesses you when you sneeze, you are not to bless them back." Saying so, the Buddha imposed upon them a precept that if someone does so, that is the end of it.

Since then, when monks sneezed the lay people would bless them. But the monks would not bless back the lay people. Because of this, people criticized the monks, saying, "While we bless the monks who have become the sons of the Sakyā lord, they do not bless us." Hearing this, the monks related this to the Buddha. Buddha, knowing this, revoked his precept, understanding that people liked to get the blessings of the monks.

Then the monks asked the Buddha, "Honorable sir, from where does this habit of blessing someone when they sneeze come?" The Buddha

---

7 The fourfold followers, or the fourfold Buddhist community, are monks [*bhikkhu*-s], nuns [*bhikkhunī*-s], laymen [*upāsaka*-s], and laywomen [*upāsikā*-s].

said, "Monks, it has been practiced for a long time." The monks asked the Buddha to relate the story. This is how it was:

At one time, King Brahmadatta was ruling in Benares. At that time, the Enlightenment Being was born the son of a businessman. This businessman used to sell glass bangles and such other fancy items. He used to send his son here and there with them to sell them and bring him back the money.

One day they came to the city of Benares. They searched for a place to spend the night, asking people where visitors could rest overnight. One person said, "Sir, there is an empty mansion on the outskirts of the city. But there is a demon living there. If you would like, though, you can go and sleep there." Then the businessman's son said, "Yes sir, we will go to that very place and sleep. I would like to tame the demon." And he requested him to show them the way to the mansion so that they might sleep there overnight.

The father and the Enlightenment Being both lay down, and the Enlightenment Being massaged his father's feet. At that moment, the demon who had worked as a slave to the demon king Vessavaṇa fetching him water and food, and who after ending his service had been given as a boon permission to eat anyone who does not bless someone upon their sneezing, as well as anyone who upon being blessed does not return a blessing, was thinking of eating the father and son. He took a little bit of dust and threw it at the reclining father's nostrils. The father sneezed. The son, who was massaging his father's feet, did not bless his father. The demon, who had been waiting in the mansion's central rafter, came down with the intention of eating him. The Enlightenment Being saw him and thought, "No doubt he is a demon who comes to eat people who do not bless after someone sneezes." Thinking so, he said, "Gagga, live a hundred years, less twenty!" So blessing his father, he requested the demon not to come near him. Leaving the son, the demon started to approach the father. The father, also seeing him, thought, "No doubt he is a demon who comes to eat people who do not return a blessing when so blessed."

And he said, "Son, you also live long – a hundred years, less twenty! As I bless you, the demon cannot come to me." As both blessed each other, the demon could not do anything, and kept silent.

Then the Enlightenment Being spoke, "Hey, demon! You have done many unwholesome deeds in the past. You have been born as you are now as a result of those unwholesome deeds. Now, also, you take the life of others. In the future, because of this, you will suffer for a long time. Therefore, you have gone from darkness to darkness." He advised him not to do evil deeds and taught him the five precepts.[8] Doing so, he tamed the demon. The next morning, he told this news to many people.

When the king heard this news, he was very pleased. He thought, "This type of person is clever in every deed." He appointed the Enlightenment Being as his commander-in-chief. He gave many gifts and presents to the Enlightenment Being's father. For the demon, he provided a respectable mansion. And he ordered the people to give the demon food and gifts. With doing so, after ruling righteously for a long time under the guidance of the Enlightenment Being, he died in accord with his Kamma [acts].

"The Venerable Ānanda, who is today the treasurer of the Dhamma, was at that time the king of Benares. The Venerable Mahā Kassapa, who is the foremost monk among those ridding themselves of defilements, was at that time the father of the Enlightenment Being. I who am the noblest of all living beings, the Buddha, was the businessman's son who tamed the demon." Saying so, the Buddha ended this story of Gagga.

The moral: "Disasters are not disasters in front of the wise."

8 For the five precepts, see note 4 above.

156

The Story of Alīnacitta [One Who Has Attained an Encouraged Mind]
(*Alīnacitta-Jātaka*)

Then again, when the lord Buddha was living in the temple of Jeta Grove, this Jātaka story was delivered about a monk who had been discouraged in his meditation. The story of the present is similar to that of the *Saṁvara-Jātaka* in the eleventh book [No. 462], where it is explained in detail.

[There was once a person who lived in Sāvatthi who heard the Buddha and, his mind being pleased, he became a monk. After this, he fulfilled his duties to his master[9] for five years. He learned what he needed to know for successful meditation, and then he left to go live alone and meditate. He went to the country of Kosala. There he came to a remote village. The villagers, seeing the monk's calm demeanor, were pleased in their minds. They requested him to stay in their village, and they made a shelter for him. They invited him to spend the rainy season retreat there. Doing so, observing the rainy season retreat there for the whole three months, he strove to meditate but he could not gain any results from this. Then he thought, "Indeed, the Buddha taught that there are four different types of people who are smart in different ways. I am one who can teach Pāli. Therefore, what is the use of staying in this remote village." Giving up his efforts to meditate, he went back to Sāvatthi to stay there, to look upon the Buddha's beauty, and to listen to his sweet words. He went to Jetavanārāma and he saw his teacher, his master, and other relatives and friends whom he knew before. When they asked why he returned, he said

9 A master is an elderly teacher of one's teacher.

that he had given up the effort to obtain *nibbāna* (final release from all existence). They all reproached him. And they took him to the Buddha. The Buddha asked them, "Oh monks, why did you bring this monk here unwillingly?" They informed the Buddha of the reason for their doing so.

Buddha said, "Oh monk, why did you give up your efforts? In my teaching it is not possible for a lazy person to attain the goal of Arahantship (sainthood). But in one of your previous lives, you have exerted a great effort."]

Buddha continued, "In the past when Benares, which was twelve Yojana-s[10] in breadth, was surrounded by enemies, you defeated them and got back the kingdom." Then the monks asked the Buddha, "Venerable sir, please reveal to us this story." And then the Buddha revealed it. This is how it was:

At one time King Brahmadatta was ruling in Benares. There were 500 carpenters living in that city. They would go to a nearby forest, and bring timber for their work. They made various types of furniture, and by selling this they earned their living.

Once, those carpenters thought, "It is difficult to bring timber from the forest. If we can go to the forest where timber is available, we can prefabricate houses there in the forest. And then we can earn a living easily." Thinking so, they started to live there in the forest.

A big elephant who lived in that forest, one day while walking, stepped on the rotting root of a tree and a piece of it stuck in the flat bottom of his foot. It was very painful. Then, going on three feet, he went to the place where the carpenters were staying. Going there, he lay down in pain. On seeing this, the carpenters came to him. And when they saw the large thorn stuck in his foot, they took it out and applied medicine to heal the wound. After several days, the wound was healed, and the elephant became very friendly with the carpenters. He thought he should pay gratitude to these carpenters, and he started to work for them by bringing heavy timbers from the forest. He then continued to live there, working for them.

---

10 1 *Yojana* = roughly 7 miles.

In this way, he worked for them bringing them timber. His food was supplied by the 500 carpenters. He ate this food supplied by the carpenters, and when he became old he thought, "Now I am weak. Therefore, I have to pay my gratitude to these carpenters by sending my intuitive and wise young son to work on my behalf."[11] And thinking so, he summoned his calf. He requested his son to work for the carpenters and to please them as he did. Giving his son to the carpenters, he went away.

Then the elephant calf worked for the carpenters, pleasing them. Also, he would play in the nearby river with their children. He became friendly with them also. Intuitive elephants like our calf do not drop their dung or urinate in water. One day there was a big rain, and a dung cake from our calf that was on the shore washed away from the root of a tree into the river. When the mahouts of Benares brought their elephants to the river to bathe them, their elephants would not go into the water because they smelled the dung cake.[12] The mahouts tried to see what the reason was for their elephants not wanting to go into the water. When they investigated, they found the dung cake. Also, they found that it was not an ordinary elephant's dung, but that it was a noble and intuitive elephant's dung.[13] Knowing this, they took it, mixed it with water, and sprinkled it over their elephants. Then the elephants smelled the fragrance of the dung, they became pleased, and they went down to the river.

The mahouts now knew that the elephant living upstream with the carpenters was an intuitive elephant, and they said to the king, "It would be good to bring him here as the royal elephant." Hearing the news, the king became very happy and organized a party to go upstream to the carpenters' camp. Finally, he decided to go with them, and they all went.

When they reached the carpenters' camp, the young elephant calf was playing in the water. He heard the music accompanying the king's

---

11 An intuitive elephant is one that knows the wishes of a mahout intuitively.

12 Elephants, in general, do not want to spend time or go where another elephant has laid its dung.

13 There are ten elephant castes. Among them, the dung of one, the next to the highest caste, is fragrant. All elephants of this caste are intuitive.

retinue, came out from the river, and went near the carpenters. The carpenters, seeing the procession, went to welcome the king. Seeing the king, they paid obeisance to him and said, "Your lordship, why do you come here? If you need any timber, all you have to do is send us a messenger." The king said, "No, no. I did not come to request timber from you. I came to request this elephant calf from you." The carpenters said, "Well, your lordship, take him and go." And then the king ordered his mahouts to take the elephant calf with them. But the elephant calf would not go. The king asked the elephant calf why it did not want to go. The carpenters said, "Your lordship, he would like you to pay us the costs we incurred in having protected and cared for him." The king estimated the costs by pricing the elephant thus: "For the trunk, 100,000 gold coins. For the four feet, 400,000 gold coins. For the tail, 100,000 gold coins." In this way, he estimated that he would give the carpenters 600,000 gold coins for the elephant. And in the presence of the elephant, he gave the money to the carpenters. The king then requested the elephant to come with them, but the elephant still would not move. The king asked again what the reason was for the elephant's not moving. The carpenters said, "Your lordship, the elephant wants you to give us 500 garments." The king ordered his servants to give the carpenters 500 garments. Even then, the elephant would not move. Again, the king asked why the elephant would not move. And the carpenters said, "Your lordship, he would like you to give garments to the wives of the 500 carpenters as well." And the king did so. Again, the elephant would not move, and the king questioned why. Then, the carpenters said that the elephant wanted the king to give gifts to their children. He did so. When he was done, without anyone saying anything, the elephant started to go on his own.[14]

Then the king of Benares, before they reached Benares with the elephant, sent forward orders to decorate Benares like the divine heaven before they arrived. With everyone having done so, the king came to

---

14 The reason the carpenters were able to talk for the elephant is that this is what they wanted all along. And the elephant was being intuitive.

Benares with the elephant. He entered the city in a procession so that the people of Benares could pay their respects to both him and the elephant.

In the course of time, the elephant became intimate with the king. Meanwhile, the Enlightenment Being was conceived in the womb of the king's queen. When it was near to the time of delivery, unfortunately the king died from a certain illness. The ministers thought that they should not tell this news of the death of the king to the elephant.

The king of Kosala, on hearing this news, sent a message to the ministers that as there was no successor to the king of Benares, therefore Benares was his. He came to the city, and surrounded it with his troops. He sent another messenger saying, "Get ready to give me the kingdom of Benares, or wage war!"

On hearing this, the king's ministers sent a message saying, "The Brahmin soothsayers have said that the queen has a boy in her womb and that she will deliver in seven days. After seven days, we will either give you the kingdom, or fight." On hearing this, the king of Kosala accepted these conditions.

After seven days, the Enlightenment Being was born. When he was born, the ministers thought, "It is not easy to fight when there is no king to give commands. Our army will have no encouragement. And the army will be routed. So we cannot fight." Therefore, they said to the queen, "Your grace, we are not powerful enough to fight as we have no king. Let us inform the royal elephant of the king's passing away. In that way, we can get the help of the royal elephant." Hearing this, the queen agreed to it. She took the Enlightenment Being in a comfortable cloth to the royal elephant and said, "Friend elephant! Your friend the king has died. We did not inform you thinking that you also would die from grief. In the meantime, the king of Kosala has come with his army and surrounded the city. This is your friend the king's son. If we fight without a leader, the king of Kosala will win and he will kill your friend the king's son. Therefore, you kill him now, and we will not fight." Saying so, she placed the baby in front of the royal elephant.

Then the royal elephant took the baby with his trunk, placed it on his head, and cried. Then he placed the baby again in the hands of its mother, and he went to fight.

The ministers caparisoned the elephant with finery, armed him with golden weapons, and scented him. He went forward and trumpeted. Then the ministers opened the four gates of the city, and all the king's elephants that had gathered at the four gates trumpeted. The enemy and his elephants, hearing this, all fled away here and there. The king of Benares' elephants trampled the camp of the king of Kosala outside the city, and the royal elephant grabbed the king of Kosala by his topknot and dragged him to the Enlightenment Being, where he left him. The ministers asked the royal elephant to kill the king of Kosala, but he did not do so. Instead, he advised the king of Kosala not to wage war again and not to kill people. And he sent him back to his own country.

The Enlightenment Being was named Alīnacitta. He was crowned king when he was seven years old. He became the king of a hundred states. He died according to his deeds [*kamma*]. While alive, he ruled righteously.

Saying so, the Buddha concluded this story, advising the monks, "Oh monks, by the energy of that elephant, the kingdom was saved for a little newborn baby. Likewise, you also should make an effort to end the suffering of life."

At the end of this preaching, the monk who had been discouraged from meditating, on hearing this discourse, attained Arahant-ship [sainthood] by the development of his mind. "The mother of the baby Enlightenment Being at that time was later to become Queen Mahāmāyā [the Buddha Gotama's mother]. The father was later to become King Suddhodana [the Buddha Gotama's father]. The intuitive elephant was this monk who was discouraged in his meditation. His father was the Venerable Sāriputta. I who am today the Buddha was at that time Prince Alīnacitta." Saying so, the Buddha concluded this Jātaka story of Alīnacitta.

The moral: "Effort is rewarded."

157

The Story of Things of Quality
(*Guṇa-Jātaka*)

When the Buddha was living at Jetavanārāma the great elder, Venerable Ānanda, was fortunate to receive a thousand robes on one day. The story of this is as follows:

One day, when the great elder Ānanda was preaching to the king of Kosala's palace women, the king of Kosala received a thousand sets of garments each worth one thousand gold coins. The king gave 500 sets of these garments to the women who were listening to the Venerable Ānanda's preaching. Those women kept these garments without wearing them, and they offered them to the Venerable Ānanda the next time he came to preach.

The great elder Ānanda received them and returned to the monastery. On the next day, at lunchtime, those 500 ladies went to take lunch with the king wearing old clothes. The king asked, "Why are you not wearing the new garments that I gave you only recently?" The ladies said, "Your lordship, we have given them to Venerable Ānanda." The king asked, "Did Venerable Ānanda himself take them all?" The ladies said, "Yes, your lordship." Then the king became upset, and said, "Buddha admonished the monks to have only three robes. By receiving such a number of garments, is he perhaps selling these robes?" And he got angry. So he went to the monastery, and asked the Venerable Ānanda, "Venerable sir, do you preach to the palace women?" And Venerable Ānanda said, "Yes, your lordship, I preach to them." Then the king asked, "Do they listen to you and learn?" And again, Venerable Ānanda said, "Yes, your lordship, they listen. And some of them even learn what I say by heart."

Then the king asked again, "Do they only listen to you, or do they give you presents as well?" The Venerable elder said, "Yes, your lordship. Yesterday they listened to the Dhamma [the teaching of the Buddha], and offered me 500 sets of garments." Then the king asked, "The omnipresent Buddha admonished you to have only three robes. Why did you accept this many sets of garments?" The Venerable elder said, "Your lordship, the omnipresent Buddha admonished us to use only three robes.[15] But he did not forbid us to receive more robes. Therefore, there is no offence. The sets of garments I received I will give to monks whose dress garments are worn out." The king said, "Then what will you do with the worn out dress robes?" Then the elder said, "Those robes will become outer robes." Then the king said, "What will you do, then, with the old outer robes?" The elder said, "We will cut out the worn areas, and use them as skirt robes." "What will you do with the old skirt robes?" "Those robes we will use as bed linen." "Then what will you do with the old bed linen?" Then the Venerable elder said, "They will be used as carpets." "Then what will you do with the old carpets?" "They will be used as doormats." "Then what will you do with the old doormats?" Then the Venerable elder said, "Your lordship, the offerings made by the faithful ought not be destroyed. So we take a sharp knife and cut the doormats into small pieces and mix these with clay and earth, which is then used in making walls when we build huts."

The king was very satisfied on hearing this explanation. He ordered his attendants to bring the remaining 500 sets of garments, and he gave them to the Venerable Ānanda. The Venerable elder Ānanda thought, "I have previously received 500 sets of garments, and now I have still another 500 sets of garments. But there are only 500 monks. Now, among them, the youngest is very attentive and obedient to me. He takes care of all my needs – cleaning, sweeping, renewing the cow dung flooring of my cell every three months as needed, providing me with food and water,

15 The three allowed robes are a two plied outer robe [*saṅghāṭī*], a two part dress robe [*uttarāsaṅga*], and a bottom skirt robe worn underneath the two part dress robe [*antaravāsaka*].

and generally working hard. So I have to treat him well." Thinking so, the Venerable elder Ānanda, being well disposed toward him, gave him the remaining 500 sets of garments.

That young monk received these sets of garments from the Venerable Ānanda and offered them in turn to the 500 monks all of whom were disciples of the Venerable Ānanda. Those 500 monks converted them into new dress garments, which they colored canary yellow. They then went to see the Buddha and asked, "Revered sir, is there among nobles who have attained the stream entrance state of mind [*sotāpanna*-s] partiality?" Then the Buddha said, "Oh monks, no such noble ones have partiality." Then they asked, "Then why has our preceptor given 500 sets of clothing to one young monk?" Then the Buddha said, "Oh young monks, this is not done by the elder Ānanda due to partiality, but rather out of gratitude to one who was very helpful to him. Not only he, but even noble ones who lived in the past have done such acts to show their gratitude." And the monks invited the Buddha to relate the past story.

The Buddha said this story:

At one time when King Brahmadatta was ruling the kingdom of Benares, the Enlightenment Being was born as a lion who lived in a cave in a certain rock. Near that rock, there was a lake along the banks of which there was an area that had been eroded. In that area, a muddy swamp had grown up with beautiful green grasses. Light animals, like rabbits and deer, were able to graze there. But heavy animals could not go there. One day, the lion who was the Enlightenment Being went to the top of his rock and looked around for food. He saw a deer grazing in the grassy swamp. He thought he would pounce on the deer. He roared, and then he pounced. On hearing the roaring noise of the lion, the deer fled quickly. The lion was not able to control the speed of his jump, and he landed with his four feet in the swamp. His four legs were stuck in the mud, and he could not free himself from this trap. For seven days he starved, with his legs stuck in the mud. Eventually, there came a jackal who on seeing the lion became afraid. He began to run away.

The lion saw the jackal and called out, "Please, do not run! Do not be afraid of me! My four feet are stuck in the mud of this swamp. Come and save my life!" The jackal approached without fear and said, "Oh lion king, I can free your lordship using a certain stratagem that I know. But I am afraid that if I do so, you will kill me. If you promise me that I can live, I will free you."

On hearing the jackal's words, the lion king said, "Hey, jackal! Do not be afraid of me. Help me get out of this place. I will not kill you. As long as you live, I will protect you. Please save me by using whatever stratagem you know."

Hearing that, the jackal dug away an area of mud from around each foot of the lion. When water flowed into these areas, the remaining mud became soft. When the mud became soft, the jackal crawled underneath the belly of the lion, and raised himself up quickly. At the same time, he had instructed the lion to make an effort to jump when he did so. The lion became released from the mud in this fashion. Then the lion sat for a while on the shore. While he was sitting there, he saw a buffalo passing by. He killed the buffalo, and he gave fresh meat to the jackal. Afterwards, he ate.

The jackal ate a little bit of meat from his share, and took the rest in his mouth to carry with him. The lion asked, "To whom do you carry this meat?" The jackal said, "Your lordship, I am carrying this to your slave who is my wife." The lion said, "O.K. Take this meat to her and come back with her. The two of you can live here near my cave." And he arranged in this way for them to live nearby. From that time on, the lion king and the jackal would hunt for food together.

When they went to hunt, the lion's wife and the she-jackal both stayed together in the same cave. The lion and the jackal would each bring a piece of meat for their spouses. In the meantime, while they were passing time in this way, the lioness gave birth to two cubs. The she-jackal also gave birth to two cubs. All the four cubs played together. The lion loved the young jackals as his own. The lioness, though, had a doubt as to these living arrangements. So, when the lion and the jackal would go out to hunt, the lioness would frighten the she-jackal saying, "Do not stay here. Flee away. It is not good for you to stay with lions." And she had her cubs frighten the young jackals.

Eventually, the she-jackal spoke to her husband and said, "The lioness frightens me when you are away, and also she has her cubs frighten our cubs. She does not know that we have been given protection by the lion." The jackal then went to the lion and said, "Your lordship, we are living here together for a long time. Therefore, there may be friction growing up between us. Your lordship's mate and cubs sometimes frighten my wife and children. There is no need to frighten us since we are timid animals. All you need do is tell us to leave, and we will do so. Please let us leave, and live on our own."

After listening to him, the lion king spoke to his mate. He said, "Hey, lioness! Do you know why I became friendly with this jackal and trust him?" She said, "No, I do not know." He said, "If so, please listen. Do you remember when at one time I was away hunting and did not come back for seven days? Do you know why I did not come back?" She again said that she did not know the reason. Then the lion king said, "If so, then listen. On that day, I pounced toward a certain deer. I made a mistake, and landed in a muddy swamp. I was stuck there, and was without food for seven days. This jackal released me. So he became my best friend, and like a relative. From today on, in whatever way I look upon him, you also must look upon him in the same way. You should not be cross with him." Starting then, the lioness and she-jackal developed a trust with one another. They lived together, trusting each other. The lion and jackal cubs also played together in a friendly fashion. Later, when their parents were dead, they remained friendly. Such friendship lasted for seven generations.

The Buddha then ended this story by expressing the four noble truths.[16]

---

16 The four noble truths are the truth of suffering in the world, the reason for suffering, the absence of suffering, and how to obtain the absence of suffering.

When Buddha ended this Dhamma sermon, some of the monks who had listened to it attained the mental state of the stream entrance state of mind. They became *sotāpanna*-s. An equal number of monks attained the mental state of once-returners [*sakadāgāmin*-s]. The same number of monks attained the mental state of non-returners [*anāgāmin*-s]. And again, the same number of monks attained sainthood [Arahant-ship], eradicating all defilements. In this way, this Dhamma sermon was delivered by the Buddha for the benefit of many.

"The jackal at that time was the Venerable Ānanda. And I who have become the Buddha who is the supreme being in the world was born then as the lion."

The moral: "A good deed deserves gratitude."

158

The Story of Suhanu [One with a Good Jaw] (perhaps, The Story of Subha [An 'Auspicious', or 'Pleasant' One])

(*Suhanu-Jātaka* or perhaps *Subha-Jātaka*)

The Buddha delivered this story while he was dwelling in the monastery in Jeta Grove about two quarrelsome monks. One of these monks lived in the city of Sāvatthi, and used to get angry and become violent. The other monk lived in a remote village and also was quarrelsome. These two monks were known by the other monks to both be quarrelsome monks. Once, the country monk came to the city of Sāvatthi.

Some young novice monks thought, "It would be good to observe how when these two monks get together they will act with one another." Thinking so, they put them both in the same room. When the two monks got together, they greeted one another, became friendly, and helped each other. Trusting one another, they lodged together very happily.

This news became known by everyone. One day, the elder monks who had assembled in the preaching hall before the Buddha's arrival were discussing this subject.

When the Buddha entered the preaching hall, he asked, "Oh monks, what were you discussing before my coming here?" The monks said, "Your Venerable sir, we were talking about the two monks who were always violent with everyone, but when meeting one another here, they were friendly with one another." The Buddha said, "Oh monks, not only today, even before they were friendly with one another when in the past they met one another." Then the monks requested the Buddha to disclose the ancient story. The Buddha thereupon disclosed the story of former times:

At one time, when Brahmadatta was ruling in Benares, the Enlightenment Being was the treasurer of the king. He was a very clever treasurer, and was skilled with regard to income to and outlays from the treasury through the selling and acquiring of horses.

While he was so engaged in such affairs, some 500 horses were brought to the city for sale. The king greedily wanted to purchase all the horses, but inexpensively. But the Enlightenment Being was a very righteous man, and he could not deal with horse dealers in an unrighteous way. So the king appointed as treasurer another minister who was formerly in charge of trade, and who was clever in trickery so as to be able to get goods at lower prices. He said to this minister, "We have in out stable a certain violent horse called Soṇa [Dog]. Put him among the horses being brought to be sold. When he is put among them, he will injure them by biting them and kicking them. Then those horses that are being sold will be wounded, and because of this they can be bought at a lower price. Delay the buying of those horses until they are wounded, when you will be able to get them at this lower price."

The new minister did this stratagem, and the horse merchant complained about this incorrect action of this minister to the Enlightenment Being. Then the Enlightenment Being said, "Do you not as well have such a violent horse in your stable?" Then the horse dealer said, "Yes, sir. We have a violent and rough horse named Suhanu."[17] Then the Enlightenment Being said, "Alright. If this is so, on your next trip, bring that horse also."

On hearing this advice, the horse dealer determined to bring that horse on his next trip. When the next trip came the king, after hearing the news of the coming of the new horses from one of his messengers went up

17 Both D. Jinaratana's and Vēragoḍa Amaramōli's editions of Virasiṁha Pratirāja's late 13th – early 14th c. C.E. Sinhala translation of the Jātaka stories, *Pansiyapaṇas Jātaka Pota*, give the horse's name here as Subha ['Auspicious', or 'Pleasant']. Ven. Pandit Widurupola Piyatissa Mahā Nāyaka Thera's edition of the 5th c. C.E. scholar Buddhaghosa's Pāli commentary on the Jātaka stories, and E. B. Cowell's English translation of the Jātaka stories, for instance, give the horse's name though as Suhanu [One with a Good Jaw].

to the top floor of the palace to see them from afar. Seeing on his own that they were coming, he released his violent horse known as Soṇa [Dog]. After being released, when the other horses approached, the two violent horses came close to one another and when they met, they put their lips together like two lovers. They became friendly, and looked lustily at one another.

The king, looking at the Enlightenment Being's face, said, "It is so strange that these two horses are looking at one another as if in lust. What is the reason for this?" Then the Enlightenment Being said, "Your lordship, when a bad man meets another bad man, they will join together even if they never knew one another before. Good men join with good men. Therefore, one rough low status horse joins together with another rough low status horse." The Enlightenment Being further stated, "Your lordship, it is not good for you to be greedy. It is not the tradition of good people to obtain wealth in an unrighteous way. That is wrong." On hearing this, the king handed back over to the Enlightenment Being his former post as treasurer.

The Enlightenment Being did the trade in a righteous way. He gave the true value of the horses to the horse dealer. The horse dealer, having obtained the proper value of his horses, returned home satisfied.

After this, the king always followed the advice of the Enlightenment Being and ruled his country righteously. In due course, he died in accord with his acquired meritorious Kamma [deeds and their accumulated consequences].

Having said this, the Buddha disclosed that those two rough and violent horses at that time are today these two monks who become violent and angry. The king was the Venerable Ānanda. The righteous minister was he himself who today has become the fully enlightened Buddha.

Preaching so, he ended this Jātaka story of Suhanu [One with a Good Jaw].

The moral: "People of a similar temperament bond together with one another."

159

The Story of a Peacock
[The Story of a Golden Peacock]
(*Mora-Jātaka, Suvaṇṇamayūra-Jātaka*)

The compassionate omnipresent one was at one time living in the monastery of Jeta Grove. At that time, there was a monk who was disheartened in his monkhood. He was taken to the enlightened one, and the enlightened one asked, "Is it true that you have become unhappy about your ordination?" The monk said, "Yes" to the Buddha. Then the Buddha asked, "What is the reason for this?" The monk responded by saying that he had seen a well-attired woman, and he was infatuated with her. That was the reason for his mind being upset. The Buddha said, "Oh, that is not a reason to be upset." He added, "Not only a dim-witted monk such as this one is infatuated by women, but also even noble ones such as Enlightenment Beings have as well been infatuated by women." Then the monks invited the Buddha to disclose the story of former times.

At one time, there was a king who was ruling Benares called Brahmadatta. At that time, the Enlightenment Being was born as a peacock. The egg from which he hatched was of a golden color. Just so, he too was born with that golden color. When he grew up, his feathers became beautified with red stripes. In this way, he became very beautiful to all who saw him. Everyone who saw him thought he was very attractive and that he had much physical beauty.

One day he thought, "My body's physical beauty is dangerous to me as long as I am living among humans." Thinking so, he flew to the Himalayan forest beyond the third range of mountains, and lived in the fourth range near the plateau of a rock in the forest called Daṇḍaka. Every day, the peacock came down to the base of the rock to get his daily food. When he got down to the base of the rock, seeing the rising sun, he uttered a spell for his protection. The sense of this spell is as follows:

"Destroying the darkness of the night,
And bringing light that spreads throughout the whole world
so that people can see forms,
Bringing the grace of light throughout the whole
universe to those who have eyes,
I worship that great sun.
Throughout today, let me be protected by that same sun
god, and let me live without fear throughout the day!"

Saying this spell after worshipping the sun god, he searched for food. And he lived without any danger.

He also recited lines of verse honoring the Buddha [of his time], the sense of which is:

"To him who has eradicated his entire
unwholesomeness,
And who has completely understood the five
aggregates, the four elements, and the six faculties, as well as
the meanings of all ends,
Having become a fully enlightened one,
To such an all-knowing one who has attained an
omnipresent state,
To him, let me pay homage!
To him who in the past has fulfilled his perfections as
an Enlightenment Being, being endowed with many virtuous
qualities,
To him, let me pay homage!
To whatever teaching such a supreme being may have
realized through his own knowledge from being a fully
enlightened one,
To that, let me pay homage!
To whatever splendid Dhamma was preached by him,

To that, let me pay homage!
To the ones who attained sainthood in the community
of the Saṅgha [clergy] by following that Dhamma,
To them, let me pay homage!
And to the members of the Saṅgha who have realized
whatever among the fourfold truths of enlightenment,
To them, let me pay homage!"

This king peacock, gaining protection by chanting this spell, then went to the feeding ground. He wandered about everywhere he might want in his range without any danger. When he returned in the evening to the plateau of the rock where he spent the night, again he recited a spell of protection. Again, the sense is as follows:

"To that same sun that is now setting down,
I pay homage!
I live being away from that glittering shine of the sun,
And I live without fear and danger in the night.
"To whatever Enlightenment Beings lived in the world
knowing the three Veda-s and knowing the entire Dhamma,
I pay homage!
Let there be homage toward the Buddha!
Let there be homage toward the entire Dhamma!
Let there be homage toward those who have attained
Arahant-ship [sainthood] and Nibbāna [release from the cycle
of birth and death]!
Let there be homage toward the Saṅgha, and toward the
emancipation those have attained!"

By reciting these stanzas of protection, the peacock passed the night safely.

In this way, he would protect himself by chanting spells of protection every day. While he was living like this, a forest hunter who was wandering throughout the Himalayan forest where the Enlightenment Being was living, saw the Enlightenment Being. After returning to his village, after many years, he said to his son when he was dying, "There is a golden colored peacock on the plateau of a rock in Daṇḍaka forest. If one day the king wants a golden peacock, go and catch him, and give him to the king." Saying this, he died.

At that time, the queen of the king of Benares, who was known as Khemā, had a dream in the night that she was listening to the Dhamma being preached by a certain golden peacock. She got up in the morning, and told the king of her dream. She said to the king, "If I do not get the chance to listen to this golden peacock preach, then I will die." Such was her craving.

The king, hearing this, summoned his ministers and asked, "Do you know of a golden peacock?" The ministers, as they had no knowledge of whether or not there was a golden peacock, said, "This will be known by the Brahmins." The Brahmins said, "That would be known by the forest hunters." Then the king summoned the forest hunters and asked, "Do you know where there are golden peacocks?"

Among those forest hunters, one said, "Your lordship, beyond the three ranges of hills in the Himalayan forest, on the plateau of a rock in the Daṇḍaka forest, there is a golden peacock." Then the king said, "If it is so, go and bring it without killing it." Then the forest hunter said, "Yes", and promising to bring it, he went home and he explained to his son in the same way that his father had explained to him the way to go to that forest. The son went, and he saw the golden peacock on the plateau of the rock in the Daṇḍaka forest. Seeing this, he made much effort to capture the golden peacock in a trap he set at the base of the rock. But he could not catch him because of the power of the spells of the Enlightenment Being. Even though the Enlightenment Being might place his foot in the trap, it did not close on it. This hunter attempted to catch the golden peacock for the remainder of his entire lifetime, and still he could not catch him. Finally, he died in the Daṇḍaka forest.

Queen Khemā was distraught at not having the golden peacock. For that reason, she also died. The king then got angry, thinking that because of the golden peacock his queen had died. The king, being very angry, had written on a golden plate that on a rock in the Daṇḍaka forest, in the Himalayan forest, there is a golden peacock. If someone eats its flesh, he will be immortal. Placing this golden plate in his treasury, the king also died.

The successor of that king saw the golden plate and, after reading it, he thought, "It would be good to become immortal by eating that golden peacock's flesh." Thinking so, he also sent a hunter. That hunter as well tried very hard to catch the peacock. But because of the power of the peacock's spells, he could not catch him.

In this way, six kings sent six forest hunters, and none of them were capable of catching the peacock. They all died in the forest.

The seventh king who came to the throne, on reading the golden plate, also sent a hunter. That hunter went to the place and tried to catch the Enlightenment Being. He also placed a trap, but he failed to catch him. He thought, "Even though this peacock placed his foot in the trap, it did not close. Why did this happen?" Thinking so, while he was trying to investigate this, one day in the morning he saw the Enlightenment Being chanting the spells and paying respects. Seeing this, the hunter thought, "If it is so, I will confound his chanting of spells." He went to a certain remote village and got a peahen. He trained her to dance and utter her cry when he snapped his fingers. He took her back to the Himalayan forest. He placed the peahen on the way of the golden peacock to his feeding range. Placing her there, before the Enlightenment Being uttered his spells, he had her dance and cry out with lustful sounds. The Enlightenment Being had not heard for a long time such a lustful cry. Hearing it and becoming possessed by devils, he became dumbly infatuated by her sound. He approached the place where the peahen was without having chanted his spells. In this way, he was captured in the hunter's trap. Then the hunter, having captured the peacock, took him to the king. The king, on seeing him, became very happy.

The peacock king questioned the king, "Why did you bring me here?" The king said, "I heard that those who eat your flesh become immortal. Therefore, I brought you here to kill you and to eat your flesh."

The peacock king said, "How can someone become immortal by eating my flesh? How can they become immortal if I myself am mortal, and am dead?" The king said, "Do not say this. Are you not the golden peacock?" Then the peacock king said, "If it is so, then listen to the reason as to how I became golden. I was a Universal Monarch in ancient times in Benares. I was practicing the five precepts[18] strictly. I ruled the country righteously. Because of all this when I died, I was born in the divine heaven. When I died there, I was born in this animal birth on account of unwholesome deeds that I had done. As I had practiced the five precepts, I became possessed of such a beautiful form."

The king did not believe this. Because of this, the peacock king said, "When I was ruling as a Universal Monarch in the ancient times, I flew by air in a golden chariot. If you want to see that chariot, go to your royal pond and bale the water out of it. At the bottom, you will find my golden chariot." Hearing this, the king did so, and baled the water out of the pond. The golden chariot was retrieved from the pond.

Seeing this, the king became very happy. He released the Enlightenment Being.

The Enlightenment Being then requested of the king that he observe the five precepts. He advised him not to kill any living being.

After saying so, he flew back to the rock in the Daṇḍaka forest.

The master Enlightenment Being having thus disclosed this, the Buddha ended the Jātaka story of the golden peacock. At the end of this Jātaka story, the monk who had become confused by craving for a woman attained Arahant-ship [sainthood], having extinguished his defilements.

The Buddha said, "The Venerable Ānanda was the king at that time. And I who am today the Buddha was the golden peacock."

The moral: "Lust is universal. Controlling one's lust is the duty of individuals."

18 For the five precepts, see note 4 above.

160

The Story of Vinīlaka [One Who is Deep Blue]

(*Vinīlaka-Jātaka*)

The lord master Gotama Buddha delivered this Jātaka story when he was living in the temple of the Bamboo Grove in the city of Rājagaha. It was delivered on an occasion when the Venerable Devadatta was professing to be as the Buddha.

Buddha had requested both chief disciples to go to Gayāsīsa and to bring back the 500 disciples that had been taken away by the Venerable Devadatta after seeing in a vision that they were capable of attaining Arahant-ship at that time. On hearing the request of the fully enlightened one, those two chief disciples went to Gayāsīsa, where Devadatta was living. When they went there, they had a chat with the Venerable Devadatta. After that, Devadatta, pretending to be like the Buddha, said to Sāriputta and Moggallāna, the two chief disciples, "My back is aching. Let me take a rest." And he lay down behind the preaching pulpit. Then the Venerable Sāriputta started to preach to the assembled 500 monks. And all 500 attained Arahant-ship. After that, they all got up and went along with the two chief disciples to see the Buddha. While Devadatta was in a deep sleep his disciple Kokālika arrived there, and he saw Devadatta sleeping there all alone. He got upset and kicked him, and then Devadatta vomited three mouthfuls of blood.

Venerable Sāriputta and Moggallāna came to see the Buddha with the 500 monks who had just attained Arahant-ship. The Buddha asked, "Oh, two chief disciples, what was Devadatta doing when you saw him?" The two chief disciples said, "Your Venerable lordship, Venerable

Devadatta behaved as if he were you. After we left, his chief disciple kicked him and caused him to vomit three mouthfuls of blood." Then the Buddha said, "Oh monks, it is not only now, but even in the past that Venerable Devadatta lost a status of splendor by pretending to be of the same status as myself." Then the monks requested the Buddha to relate that story. And the Buddha disclosed the hidden story:

At one time, there was a king called Videha in the city of Mithilā in the country of Videha. At that time, a certain golden swan had sexual relations with a crow. As a result of that relationship, the crow had a son. He was not as dark as his mother, nor was he a golden color as was his father. He was the color of neither of his parents, but was a deep blue. Therefore, his parents named him Vinīlaka [One Who is Deep Blue].

The father swan had also two children in the Himalayan Mountains. From time to time, the swan would come to the city of Mithilā to see this son. His two other children said one day, "Father, it is not good for you to go to the city where human beings live. By doing so, you may come upon danger. Therefore, let the two of us go to the city and bring back here your other son."

Then the father swan said, "In that case, go to the city of Mithilā. Near the royal palace, there will be a certain Palmyra tree with a crow's nest in it. Both of you go, and bring him." Saying so, the father swan bid his two children to go.

The two young swans went there and saw the crow called Vinīlaka. They talked with him, and became friendly with him. Having him perch on a stick, they flew over the middle of the city toward the Himalayan forest holding the stick in their beaks.

At that same time King Videha, who had been adorned beautifully by his retinue, had gotten into a chariot drawn by four white horses and was going around the city so as to display his grandeur. In the meantime, Vinīlaka was being carried by the two young swans. Seeing the grandeur of the king, he said, "The king who rules while sitting in the palace of the kingdom of Mithilā comes through the city in a chariot drawn by four white horses. And I myself, going by air, am in a chariot drawn by two golden swans."

Hearing these words, the two young swans got angry. They thought of killing Vinīlaka right there. But then they thought again. If they did so their father would doubt their words, thinking that they did so out of jealousy. So they carried him to their father and told him about the crow's words. The golden swan got very angry and said, "Do you not understand your position? You deserve to stay in a place where dirty things such as excreta are dumped." And he ordered his two other children to take Vinīlaka back to his mother's nest and to then return. The two golden swans did so.

The Buddha, having said this, ended 'The Story of Vinīlaka'. He said, "Vinīlaka was Devadatta at that time. The two golden swan children are today the two chief disciples of the Buddha. The father was the Venerable Ānanda. King Videha was I, the Buddha who has attained holy enlightenment." In this way, the Buddha related the past story to the present.

The moral: "Conceit can destroy one's happiness."

161

The Story of Indasamānagotta [The Story of Indagotta]

(Indasamānagotta-Jātaka, Indagotta-Jātaka)

This story was delivered by the lord Buddha while he was living in Jetavanārāma on an occasion when one disobedient monk did something wrong. This disobedient monk behaved in a bad way, and it was told to the Buddha. The Buddha summoned him and questioned him, "Oh monk, were you disobedient?" The monk responded, "Yes." Then the Buddha said, "Oh monk, because of your disobedience in the past, you were once trampled by an elephant." Then the other monks requested the Buddha to disclose the story.

At one time, when King Brahmadatta was ruling in the city of Benares, the Enlightenment Being was the chief of 500 ascetics who lived in the Himalayan forest.

At that time, a certain ascetic called Indasamānagotta [or, Indagotta] was bringing up an elephant calf. The Enlightenment Being, on seeing this elephant calf, understood that when it became mature, it might bring them trouble. Seeing this, he advised Indasamānagotta not to bring him up, but to let him go alone into the forest. But the anchorite did not heed him.

As time passed, the elephant became mature. When he was mature, as happens with elephants, he went into rut. At this time, the group of ascetics had gone to a nearby village. When they returned, they saw the elephant that was intoxicated with rut, and was violent minded. The elephant had broken up the temple, and had trampled their small huts, their watersheds, and the slabs of rock that they would sit on when meditating. All of this had been destroyed by him, and he was waiting to kill them on their return. Seeing this, they did not approach. But the ascetic who had brought him up came near to him without doubt. The elephant, seeing the ascetic who came near to him, attacked him with his tusks and killed him. He then ran off into the forest. The ascetics who witnessed this incident reported it to the Enlightenment Being. Then the Enlightenment Being organized a funeral for this ascetic. After the funeral, he summoned all the ascetics and said, "Indasamānagotta, without paying attention to my advice, had a close association with a being who was unreliable and did not behave well, and therefore came to this unexpected fate. Therefore, it is not good to make a close association with friends who are unreliable and do not behave well [*asappurisa*-s].[19] Indasamānagotta's bringing up of an elephant was the cause of his death. Therefore, you should follow the advice of reliable friends. Thereby, you will achieve the goals for which you strive."

In this way the chief ascetic, who was the Enlightenment Being, advised them. In the course of time, he passed away. The Buddha thus ended this Jātaka story of Indasamānagotta.

"The ascetic Indasamānagotta at that time was the disobedient monk of today. The chief ascetic who taught the 500 anchorites was I, who have become the fully enlightened one." Saying so, the Buddha concluded this Jātaka story.

The moral: "Association with friends who do not behave well and who are unreliable causes calamity for a person."

19 An *asappurisa* is a person who does not behave well [righteously] and who is untrustworthy, an ignoble, low person; literally, a person who is out of accord with the 'true', or created and ordered existence.

162

The Story of Intimacy
(*Santhava-Jātaka*)

The Buddha, who was helpful to people without help, while living in Jetavanārāma delivered this Jātaka story with regard to naked Jain ascetics [Nigaṇṭha-s] who were worshipping the fire god. The present circumstances of delivering this story are the same as in the *Naṅguṭṭha-Jātaka* above [No. 144] At this time, the monks in the presence of the Buddha asked his lordship, "Venerable sir, is there any advantage for these people in making offerings to the fire gods?". The Buddha said, "Oh monks, in ancient times even some noble ones abandoned the practice of sacrificing to the fire gods." The monks then requested the Buddha to disclose the ancient story.

The Buddha said:

At one time in the city of Benares, there was a king called Brahmadatta. At that time, the Enlightenment Being was born in a Brahmin family. His parents preserved the fire that was at home when the child's birth took place. They preserved it, not letting it die out. When the Enlightenment Being became sixteen years old, they said to their son, "Oh dear son, we preserved this fire from the day of your birth. If you would like, take it with you to the forest, sacrifice to it, and practice asceticism there. If not, learn the three Veda-s, marry a young girl, and lead a domestic life."

The Enlightenment Being said, "I want nothing to do with the life of a householder." He took the fire, went into the forest, and sacrificed to the god of fire while living in the forest.

At a certain occasion, he received as alms certain milk rice that was mixed with a lot of ghee. He thought, "Let me offer the first portion of milk rice mixed with ghee to my beloved fire god." Thinking so, and first making the fire big, he sprinkled the milk rice into the fire. As there was plenty of ghee mixed with it, the fire suddenly became very big and shot up. And because of that, it started to burn his hermitage. The Enlightenment Being went a distance from the hermitage and reflected, "Because of my association with this wicked fire, I have lost my hermitage that I had constructed myself alone with much effort. By association with the fire, I got only this result." Abandoning his burnt down hermitage, he retreated into the forest.

On his way, in the forest he saw four animals, a lion, a tiger, a panther, and a langhur. He noticed that the langhur was licking the faces of the three carnivorous animals. These three animals, even though they were carnivorous, because of their intimacy were not harming the monkey. On the other hand, his fire, with which he had been intimate, being evil, had harmed him instead of helping him.

Thinking so, he gave up his life in that forest, and went to the Himalayan forest, ordained himself as a holy man, and started to meditate. Through meditation, he developed his mind, and gained the five higher knowledges [*pañcābhiññā*][20] and the eightfold concentrations [*aṭṭhasamāpatti*].[21] At the end of this life, he was born in the Brahma realm.

Saying so, the Buddha ended this Jātaka story of intimacy, saying further that he, the Buddha, was the ascetic at that time.

The moral: "Blindly following what people say leads to wasted effort."

20 The five higher knowledges are miraculous powers [*iddhividhā*], the divine ear [*dibbasota*], thought reading [*paracittavijānana*], knowledge of reminiscence of former lives [*pubbenivāsānussati*(-*ñāṇa*), and clairvoyance [*dibbacakkhu*].

21 The eightfold concentrations are the four *jhāna*-s [the series of mental absorptions in meditation] and the four higher *jhāna*-s [the realm of the infinity of space, the realm of the infinity of consciousness, the realm of nothingness, and the realm of neither consciousness nor unconsciousness].

163

The Story of Susīma
(*Susīma-Jātaka*)

The omnipresent one, who became like a diamond cage protecting against evil for those who came to his refuge, delivered this Jātaka story on an occasion when there was a dispute between followers of the Jina [Nigaṇṭha-s] and the followers of the Buddha over to whom to give alms.

At one time, the inhabitants of the city of Sāvatthi used to offer alms to the Buddha, sometimes by individual family, sometimes by groups of four or five families together, sometimes by a whole street of people, and sometimes by the whole city. One time when the whole city organized to give alms, the people who were not followers of the Buddha suggested giving the alms to the followers of Nigaṇṭhanāthaputta, Makkhalighosāla, and such others from among the six types of naked ascetics. While those who had such incorrect views wanted to give alms to such Nigaṇṭha ascetics, the followers of the Buddha wanted to give the alms to the Buddha and his disciples. Engaged in this argument, they could not come to a decision for days. Then a certain wise man said, "We should give the alms to the side that has the majority." When the decision was finally made on this basis, the majority was on the side of giving the alms to the Buddha. So it was decided, and the alms giving proceeded for a period of time.

At that time, some people wanted to stop the alms giving, but the others did not let them. One day the Buddha, after the offering of alms, preached in the city and then returned to Jetavanārāma. And the monks also returned to their chambers at Jetavanārāma, and in the evening they assembled in the preaching hall. They started to talk about the way in which it was decided to give these alms. One monk said, "Oh brothers, followers of the naked ascetics tried to stop the alms giving to the Buddha and to us, his disciples, but they could not do it." While they were talking about this, the Buddha entered the preaching hall. He questioned, "Oh monks, before my arrival, what were you talking about?" The monks disclosed their conversation. Then the Buddha said, "Oh monks, not only today but also in the past, people tried to prevent me from receiving alms, but they failed to do so." The monks requested the omnipresent one to disclose the past story.

The Buddha then related the past story:

At one time, there was a king called Susīma who was ruling in Benares. He had an advisor in spiritual and secular matters [a *purohita*] who was well versed in the three Veda-s and in elephant lore.[22] As he was so well educated, each year he earned a great amount of gold and jewelry by performing sacrifices for the well-being of elephants. At that time, the Enlightenment Being was conceived in the womb of that Brahmin's wife. Seven or eight years after his birth his father, the king's Brahmin advisor, passed away.

There came then the time for the ceremony of blessing the elephants. The king's other Brahmins got together and complained to the king, "Your lordship, the time for the ceremony of blessing the elephants has come. But what are we to do, as your lordship's chief advisor has died? We do not know how to perform it properly, but neither does his son who is not at all educated. Shall we do it to the best of our ability?" The king agreed to this. Then the Brahmins set the date for the ceremony four days from that time. And they went about boasting here and there that they were going to perform the sacrifice for the well-being of the elephants and would receive therefrom much gold and jewelry. This was heard by the Enlightenment Being's mother.

22 See Franklin Edgerton, *The Elephant-lore of the Hindus*, 1931, which is an introduction and translation, with notes, of the at present best available work on elephantology, the *Mātaṅgalīlā* of Nīlakaṇṭha. Ancient Indian literature gives evidence of elephant trainers' manuals, known as *hastisūtra*-s [Sūtra-s treating elephants], and the art of training elephants [*hastiśikāā*].

Having heard this, she came home and started to cry. She moaned, "This ceremony has been performed by our family for the last seven generations. Now, because of my husband's death, we have lost that inheritance. And also, we have lost all the wealth that comes from it."

In the meantime, her son came home. He asked his mother, "Why are you crying?" She told him the reason for her grief. On hearing the reason, he said, "Mother, when are they going to perform this sacrificial ceremony?" She said, "On the fourth day from today." Then he asked, "Mother, who in this region knows the three Veda-s and the specifics of the sacrificial ceremony for the well-being of elephants." She said, "It is known only by the foremost teacher in the university that is in the city of Takkasilā, 120 Yojana-s away." He said, "Then I will go tomorrow to the city of Takkasilā to see him, and I will learn the three Veda-s and the elephant lore within two days. I will return on the third day. On the fourth day, I will perform the sacrificial ceremony for the blessing of the elephants. Therefore, do not worry." Saying so, he consoled his mother. Early the next morning he took his breakfast, and taking with him the money to pay the teacher, he left for Takkasilā. In the evening, the Enlightenment Being reached Takkasilā, having traversed the 120 Yojana-s. Once there, he went to see the foremost teacher of the university who was well versed in the three Veda-s and in elephant lore.

The teacher asked him, "Why did you come here?" The Enlightenment Being said, "I came to learn the three Veda-s and elephant lore quickly and as soon as possible." The master said, "How can I teach you such a long teaching in only a short time?" Then the Enlightenment Being said, "The performance of the sacrificial ceremony for the benefit of the elephants will take place on the third day from today. Therefore, I came here, traversing 120 Yojana-s in one day, to learn without delay. Teach me the rudiments tonight. I will learn the details later myself." The teacher agreed to teach him that night.

After the Enlightenment Being had his dinner, he went to wash the feet of the teacher. Having paid his respects to the teacher, he gave the teacher the thousand gold coins that he had brought with him.

During the course of the night the teacher taught him all that he knew. When he had finished, it was morning. The Enlightenment Being understood all that he had been taught in a single hearing. Having learnt by heart the three Veda-s and the elephant lore, he asked the teacher, "Is there any more that you have to teach me?" The teacher said, "No. That is all." When he said this, the Enlightenment Being said, "Then if that is so, I must point out errors in this and that place. Those must be corrected by you when you teach others." That morning, the Enlightenment Being left to return home. In the evening, he reached Benares and told his mother that he had learnt everything that he needed to know to perform the sacrifice.

On the day of the ceremony, there was a procession of a hundred elephants caparisoned with gold and richly ornamented and armored shrouds, mounted by mahouts carrying banners decorated with gold and silver threads and ornaments, the king's retinue carrying many other decorations, and gold and silver lances, swords, parasols, and so forth. The king's Brahmins, all decked out, also came with the intention of celebrating the sacrificial ceremony of the blessing.

The king, himself decorated with the appropriate finery for the occasion, came to the sacrificial ground. At the same time, the Enlightenment Being also came to the sacrificial ground wearing appropriate finery as well, and surrounded by his retinue. When he saw the king, he said, "Your lordship, I have heard that you have taken away my inheritance from my father of performing the sacrificial ceremony with the hundred black elephants endowed with ivory tusks and caparisoned with gold and richly ornamented and armored shrouds. Is this true?"

The king said, "Yes, my son, I have done so because you do not know how to perform the proper sacrificial ceremony as you are not well educated." The Enlightenment Being said, "Your lordship, for seven generations my family has performed this sacrifice for you and your forebears, and no one else has done it. Therefore, I can perform it better for you than all your other Brahmins, and all other Brahmins anywhere in Jambudīpa.[23] If any other Brahmin thinks he can perform it better, let him say so. None of them know the three Veda-s and the lore of elephants better than I do."

The Brahmins who were assembled there, on hearing the Enlightenment Being speak in this way with such a lion's roar, dared not speak even a word against him. After this, the Enlightenment Being was given the opportunity to perform the ceremony. After the ceremony, having collected all the riches, the Enlightenment Being went home.

The Buddha thus ended this Jātaka story.

"The mother of the Enlightenment Being at that time was the Buddha's present mother, Queen Mahāmāyā. His father at that time was the Buddha's present father, King Suddhodana. Susīma, the king of Benares, was the Venerable Ānanda. The foremost teacher who taught the Enlightenment Being was the Venerable Sāriputta. The Brahmin prince was I, the Buddha, who has attained enlightenment."

At the end of this Jātaka story, many people attained the stream entrance state of mind. They became *sotāpanna*-s. An equal number attained the state of mind of once-returners [*sakadāgāmin*-s]. And an equal number attained the state of mind of non-returners [*anāgāmin*-s]. Still an equal number attained sainthood [Arahant-ship], becoming saints [*arahant*-s] by eradicating all defilements in their minds. Therefore, this teaching was very successful for a very many people.

The moral: "Deserving people get what they deserve."

23 That is, India of the Buddha's time.

164

The Story of a Vulture
(*Gijjha-Jātaka*)

The entirely auspicious omnipresent one while he was living in Jetavanārāma delivered this Jātaka story regarding a certain monk who was supporting his parents. The present story for this is similar to the present story of the *Sāma-Jātaka* [No. 540] regarding a monk who was helping his parents.

[In the city of Sāvatthi, there lived a wealthy family that was endowed with 80 million gold coins. They had a son who was very much loved by his parents. One day, he was looking out a window and saw in the street people going in a certain direction carrying flowers, incense, perfumes, and lights. It seems that they were going to Jetavanārāma to listen to a sermon about the Dhamma (the law). On seeing them, he also decided to go to Jetavanārāma and hear the Dhamma. Going there, he offered things that he had carried with him, flowers, incense, perfumes, and lights, to the monks and to the Buddha. He sat down on the side of the assembled congregation and listened to the Buddha's words. After hearing what the Buddha said, he decided to become a monk, considering the disadvantages of lay life and the value of monkhood. He got up from where he was sitting and approached the Buddha, requesting to become a monk. The Buddha asked whether or not he had parents. He said, "Yes, I have parents." Then the Buddha said to him that he had to have permission from his parents to become a monk. He went back to his parents' home and requested the permission. His parents said, "No" to him. So he fasted for seven days, and he was then able to get the permission from his parents. He returned to the Buddha and said that he had gotten the permission to be ordained. The Buddha then summoned some capable monks, and he asked them to ordain the young man. After his ordination, he became well respected and was fortunate to get all the perquisites required for a monk. In the course of a few years, his teachers became very satisfied with all he had learnt, and he was conferred with a higher ordination. He then spent another five years under the guidance of his teachers, as required. After that, he wanted to practice meditation in the forest so as to gain insight. He went to a remote village, and lived in the forest nearby. He spent twelve years living like this, yet he could not attain any kind of a higher goal.

After his ordination, both his father and mother became poorer and poorer. Whatever they had in land and property, as well as parts of businesses, were taken away by the people who worked them, by their renters, and by their partners, because there was no one in the family who could make them give the family its due share. The slaves and workmen in the house also abandoned the family, looting whatever they could.

Finally, the father and mother were left alone by everyone, and there was no one to give them even a cup of water. As there was no one to help them, they sold the house. And as they had no possessions any longer, they became homeless beggars with dirty rags as clothing. They were wandering beggars who went in the streets from home to home begging alms.

In the meantime, a monk from Jetavanārāma in Sāvatthi left searching for a forest hermitage, and reached eventually his hermitage. The monk received him, welcoming him, and they began to talk. He was asked, "From where do you come?" The visiting monk responded, "I come from Jetavanārāma." The monk living in the hermitage inquired about the Buddha and the 80 foremost monks. Finally he asked, thinking that he would find out about his parents, "Venerable sir, do you know anything about such-and-such a family of Sāvatthi?" The visiting monk said, "Your reverence, do not ask me about them." The hermitage monk said, "Bhante, why do you say that?" The visiting monk said, "That family had a son. The son was ordained. Since then, that family's wealth and possessions little by little became less. Now they are alone, and they are living begging alms." The hermitage monk, on hearing these words of the visiting monk, could not bear it and started to cry with tears in his eyes. The visiting monk asked, "Why are you crying?" Then the hermitage monk said, "Your Venerable sir, those two are my parents. I am their son who was ordained."

The visiting monk said, "Brother, because you left your family and became ordained, your parents have come to ruin. Go and help them." Then the hermitage monk thought, "Though I have spent twelve years at meditation, I could not gain any kind of fruitful result. Therefore, I am an unworthy person. What advantage do I have on account of ordination? I will put aside my robe, and become a householder and support my parents. Doing so, I can practice generosity, morality, and do other meritorious deeds, and I can thereby attain heaven." Thinking so, he passed along his forest hermitage to the visiting monk. On the second day, he left the hermitage and went back to the city of Sāvatthi. In the course of time, he came to a fork in the road. One was toward Jetavanārāma, and the other was toward his parents' home. He thought, "To which should I go first? Should I first see my parents, or the Buddha?" Again, he thought, "I saw my parents for many years. I have only rarely seen the Buddha. And from now on, my seeing the Buddha will be very rare. First I will go to see the Buddha, and listen to him preach. Tomorrow, I will go to see my parents." Thinking so, leaving the road to his parents' home, he arrived at Jetavanārāma in the evening.

On that day the great compassionate Buddha, out of his great compassion, on coming out of his concentration saw the world, and saw this monk who had sufficient virtue to attain the stream entrance state of mind (*sotāpatti*). When this monk arrived, the Buddha was preaching the *Mātuposaka Sutta*[24] and explaining the value of parents and being grateful to one's parents. He listened from the side of the assembly.

24 See *Saṁyuttanikāya*, 'The Brahmin Suttas: The Lay Adherents, The Mother-maintainer', VII, 2, §9, as in C. A. F. Rhys Davids and Sūriyagoḍa Sumaṅgala Thera, *The Book of Kindred Sayings [Saṃyutta-Nikāya] or Grouped Suttas*, Part I, *Kindred Sayings with Verses [Sagāthā Vagga]*, [1917]: 230.

Listening, he thought, "I thought that I should maintain my parents by being a householder. But the Buddha advises that as an ascetic I can do the same thing. If I had gone to see my parents without first seeing the Buddha I indeed would have had to lose my monkhood. Now I will be able to maintain my parents without being a householder."

Thinking so, he spent the night in Jetavanārāma, and on the second day very early in the morning he went toward his parents' house in Sāvatthi. He wondered whether he should collect some gruel or see his parents first. As it would not be good to go empty-handed to poor people, he decided to get some gruel first. Then, he went toward his former house. He saw his parents lying down beside the wall opposite their former home, which they were doing after having searched unsuccessfully for gruel. He recognized his parents and became very sad. With tearful eyes, he looked at them. But his parents did not recognize him.

His mother thought that he must be a monk who had come searching for alms. She said, "Bhante, we have nothing to give you. Please go elsewhere." Hearing his mother's words, as his heart was very sad and his eyes were filled with tears, he remained standing in the same spot. She said the same thing to him for a second time, and then a third time, but he remained standing in the same spot without moving.

His father then said to his mother, "Dear, he must be your son. Go and see him." The mother got up and approaching him, she recognized him, and fell down at his feet and cried. The father then did the same. The monk also could not control himself, and he too cried. He said, however, "Do not cry. I will support you and look after you. I will bring you food from my alms." And from that time forward, he brought them a portion of his alms and maintained them. He also requested that they no longer wander, but stay in one place. He brought whatever he got. And giving them the main portion, he would eat the remainder. The clothing that he received, he gave to them. And their discarded clothing he washed, and made it into robes for himself to wear. There were more days when he got no food, though, than when he got food. His robes also became very tattered. Maintaining his parents in this way, he managed to continue living as a monk. But he became very pale and lean.

His fellow monks saw him and asked, "Venerable brother, formerly you looked so handsome. But now you look pale, and your body is lean. Are you suffering with a disease?" He said, "Brethren, I have no disease. But I have a certain hindrance." And he explained the plight of his life. The monks who heard this said, "Brother, you are doing a wrong thing by receiving alms and giving them to people who do not deserve to get them, because they were given by people who have confidence (*saddhā*) in the Dhamma." Hearing these words, he shrank, becoming very ashamed. A certain monk who heard about this and became very upset, went to the Buddha and complained, "Venerable sir, such-and-such a monk is maintaining some householders by giving them the alms given by the faithful."

The Buddha then summoned the monk and asked, "Is it true that you are maintaining lay people by giving them the food that you obtain as alms?" The monk said, "Yes, your reverence. I am doing so. That is how I look after my invalid parents." Then the lord who was a son to the human and divine world appreciated his deed, and wishing to disclose one of his previous life stories, said three times, "Monk, well done, indeed (*sādhu, sādhu, sādhu*). You have traveled the same path that I have in the past." In this way, he encouraged the maintenance of all parents with gratitude. That monk then became more motivated.]

The Buddha said, "You have done well by helping parents. Even in the past, this path was taken by noble ones." Then the monks invited the Buddha to disclose the story of old.

At one time when King Brahmadatta was ruling in Benares, the Enlightenment Being was born as a vulture on Mount Gijjhakūṭa [Vulture's Peak]. He supported his elderly parents.

At that time, there occurred a period of severe rain and wind. The two old vultures were not able to perch on the rock. They flew off to Benares with difficulty, their feathers getting very wet on the way. Meanwhile, the millionaire of Benares had gone to a nearby lake to take a bath. He saw these two old vultures who had fallen down and were unable to fly any further. Seeing them, he asked some of his servants to bring fire and he made them warm. He also sent some of his servants to the place where dead water buffaloes were being cremated to bring some unburned water buffalo meat, which he then gave them to eat.

Those vultures, after the snowy season, went back to Gijjhakūṭa. There, they told all the other vultures how the millionaire of Benares had supported them. They said, "We must be very grateful to him. How can we show our gratitude to one who has done such a great service by supporting us? Let us get for him an ornament, or some kind of cloth, and put it near his residence." Since then, whenever all these vultures saw in the street any ornament or cloth, they swooped down, took it, and put it on the millionaire of Benares' balcony.

The millionaire knew that these things were being given him by vultures. Thinking that they belonged to the vultures, he took them and stored them in a room in his residence. Meanwhile, the people of the city complained about this to the king. The king ordered them to capture a vulture, so he could question him. The people obeyed, and placed traps about the city. The vulture who helped his parents was caught in one of the traps. The man who had put out that trap took the vulture, and brought him to the king. The millionaire of Benares saw him bringing him to the king, and thought, "It would be a terrible thing if he were to be killed." So he hurried to the king's palace. In the palace, the king asked the vulture, "Are you robbing people of these things?" The vulture said, "Yes, your lordship." Then the king asked, "To whom do you give them?" The vulture said, "We are giving them to this millionaire to show our gratitude as he has helped us a great deal." Then the king became happy, and he asked, "You can see corpses from a hundred Yojana-s away. Why did you not see this trap?" The vulture said, "Yes, your lordship, vultures can see corpses a hundred Yojana-s in the distance. That is true. But, when there is a danger, it is not so easy to be seen. When a disaster lies ahead, it is not easily seen by the person who is the victim."

Then the king asked the millionaire, "Is it true that these vultures have given you this wealth?" He said, "Yes, your lordship. Please release that vulture. I will give them back all the wealth they brought me, so they can return it to the proper people."

The Buddha then ended this Jātaka story, relating the story of the past to the present.

"The king of Benares at that time was the Venerable Ānanda. The millionaire of Benares was the Venerable Sāriputta. The vulture who supported his parents was I who am now the Buddha, the fully enlightened one."

At the end of this preaching, that monk who supported his parents attained the stream entrance state of mind [*sotāpatti*], which state can be fulfilled by a thousand ways of performing Dhamma.

The moral: "It is good to support the infirm. Those who do so will receive thankfulness."

165

The Story of a Mongoose
(*Nakula-Jātaka*)

The Buddha who was compassionate toward the suffering of all people delivered this Jātaka story with regard to two officers who were always angry with one another. The present story is similar to that mentioned before in the *Uraga-Jātaka* [No. 154]. The Buddha said, "Oh monks, these two officers' anger has been removed by me even in the past." The monks then invited the omnipresent one to tell them the story.

The Buddha said:

At one time, when King Brahmadatta was ruling the city of Benares, the Enlightenment Being was born in a Brahmin family. He understood the disadvantages of living a lay life enjoying the five sensual desires,[25] and he renounced lay life and became an ascetic. He lived in a hermitage in the Himalayan Mountains. Near the hermitage, at the end of the walk that he used to circumambulate his hermitage, there was a termite hill. There a mongoose lived. Near that was a hollow tree, and in that tree there lived a snake. The mongoose and the snake were constantly biting each other and fighting. The ascetic thought, "With such a person as myself being here it is not good to let them stay like this, being angry with each other all the time." Thinking so, he advised them not to fight with one another, and he reconciled them.

One day while the snake went in search of prey, the mongoose put his head out through the termite hole with his mouth wide open, showing his sharp teeth, and was sleeping. The ascetic saw this, and came near to him and said, "The snake that was an enemy to you has become a friend.

---

25 The five sensual desires are the desires that arise from sight, hearing, smelling, tasting, and touching.

And you are now a friend of his. Why are you lying there with your mouth open showing your fearful teeth?"

The mongoose said, "Your worship, it is good to be suspicious of your friend the same as your enemy. Therefore, if your enemy becomes a friend, you must also be suspicious of him."

Then the Enlightenment Being said, "Even though you are suspicious of him, the snake harbors no bad intentions toward you." Saying so, the ascetic went away and meditated. He was successful in meditation, and attained mental absorption [*jhāna*]. After he passed away, he was born in the Brahma world. The mongoose and the snake passed away and went to their next worlds according to their deeds [*kamma*].

The Buddha saying this, he ended this story of a mongoose [*Nakula-Jātaka*]:

"The two angry officers of today were the mongoose and the snake at that time. And I who am the Buddha who has attained full enlightenment was the ascetic."

The moral: "When anger arises, it is very hard to control it."

166

The Story of Upasāḷha
(*Upasāḷha-Jātaka*)

When the fully enlightened Buddha who was a treasure of compassion for all beings was living in the Bamboo Grove monastery, there was a Brahmin called Upasāḷha living in Rājagaha. One day Upasāḷha summoned his son and said, "Whenever I die, please remember not to cremate me in a place where outcaste people are cremated. Cremate me in a clean and pure place."

The son, on hearing this, said, "Father, I do not know of such a place. If you can show me such a place, I would like to cremate you there." On hearing that, the Brahmin father said, "If what you say is true, let us go to the summit of Vulture's Peak." And together they went to Vulture's Peak. There they saw a certain place surrounded by three rocks. In the middle, there was a small empty bit of land. The Brahmin father pointed out that spot for him to be cremated on after he died. And the son agreed to do so. They then began to return home. At the same time the Brahmin father and son were descending Vulture's Peak, the Buddha was attaining to the state of great compassion [*mahākaruṇā-samāpatti*] and was looking at the world to see who needed the help of the Buddha. The Buddha saw the good fortune of acquired meritoriousness of the Brahmin father and his son such that they might attain the stream entrance state of mind [*sotāpatti*]. Seeing this, the Buddha went to climb up Vulture's Peak.

At that time, the Buddha met the Brahmin father and his son descending from the peak. He asked, "Where did you go, that you are coming down now?" The Brahmin father did not reply. But the son replied to the Buddha, "Your lordship, my father wanted me to cremate him when he died in a place where no outcaste person had been cremated. Therefore, we went to see such a place at the summit of Vulture's Peak. We saw at the top of the summit three rocks in the middle of which there was such a place. We agreed that I would cremate him there." Then the fully enlightened one said, "I would like to go and see the place. Let us go and see where that pure place is." And the three of them ascended the rock. On seeing the spot, the Buddha asked, "You and your father were searching for an uncontaminated place?" The son responded, "Yes." The Buddha said, "This is not a clean place." Then the Brahmin father spoke, and said, "Why is it so?" The Buddha explained the story of the past:

At one time, in the city of Rājagaha, there was a Brahmin called Upasāḷha. He said to his son that when he died, he should not be cremated in a place where someone had been cremated before. They went to Vulture's Peak.

At that time, the Enlightenment Being had been born in Magadha in a Brahmin family. He took his education with the foremost teacher in his region. After finishing his education, he became an ascetic with the power of reading thoughts. He lived then in the forest. When the Brahmin and his son were coming down Vulture's Peak, he was ascending. Seeing the father and son descending, he asked them what they were doing. They told him the story. The ascetic said, "Oh Brahmin, on this spot that you selected as a pure place, countless beings were both buried and cremated before. Among them was your father himself, also named Upasāḷha in each birth, who was cremated here in 14,000 births. Therefore, not only is this not a clean place but just so, it is not easy to find a clean place where a dead body has not been cremated anywhere in the world. Saying so, he went away and meditated on the four sublime states of mind.[26] At the end of his life, he was born in the Brahma world.

The Buddha saying this, he concluded the story:

26 The four sublime states of mind are loving kindness [*mettā*], compassion [*karuṇā*], sympathetic joy [*muditā*], and equanimity [*upekkhā*].

"The Brahmin and his son at that time were the same as the Brahmin father and his son today. And the ascetic at that time was I who am today the fully enlightened Buddha."

Hearing this story, the Brahmin father and his son attainted the stream entrance state of mind [*sotāpatti*] that is endowed with a thousand kinds of knowledge.

The moral: "The world is common to all."

167

The Story of Samiddhi [The Magnificent One]
(*Samiddhi-Jātaka*)

Furthermore, the omniscient one who enlightened the world was living near the city of Rājagaha in the temple called Tapodārāma [The Temple of the Hot Water Spring].[27] He delivered this sermon on account of a Venerable monk called Samiddhi. The name Samiddhi was given him because once, when he was taking a bath in the water of Tapodārāma, he was wearing his underskirt while leaving bare the upper part of his body so as to let it dry off. Many monks saw him and thought that he was very handsome looking. They gave him the name Samiddhi because he was endowed with such physical beauty.

In the meantime, a certain divine nymph, on seeing his physical beauty, fell in love with him. Becoming infatuated, she went to him and said, "Handsome sir, you are endowed with such great physical beauty, have very dark hair, and are in your youth. What is the use of living as a monk without experiencing the five sensual desires?[28] What is the use of wasting your youth? You can become a monk when you are an old man. Enjoy your youth." The monk said, on hearing her words, "Why should I be a householder? Death can come at any time, without warning. Therefore, it is not advisable to disrobe from my monk's garments and become a householder." He said to the divine damsel, "I do not wish to lay down my monk's robe." Then the

---

27 Daily, thousands of people still visit Tapodārāma to take a bath. The water is still hot.

28 For the five sensual desires, see note 25 above.

divine damsel understood his intention, and she went away.[29] And he went to the Buddha, and informed him what had transpired.

The enlightened one said, "This divine damsel spoke in this way not only to you now, but in previous lives she also spoke in this way to other noble ones." The monks who heard this requested the virtuous one to disclose how it was. Then the Buddha told this story to disclose how it happened:

At one time, there was a king called Brahmadatta ruling in Benares. The Enlightenment Being was an ascetic in the Himalayan forest. One day he went to a certain lake and took a bath. In order to let the water on his body dry off, he held his bark garment in his hand. In the meantime, a divine nymph saw the beauty of his body. Infatuated with him, she came to him and asked, "Why are you living in this way without enjoying the five sensual desires? Why cannot you perform asceticism when you become old? This is not the time to be an ascetic. This is the time to live a householder's life." On hearing these words, he said, "Hey, unwise one. No one knows when he or she will die. Because of this, I am practicing asceticism at this time. I will never give up my ordination as an ascetic." Then the divine damsel became very upset, and became embarrassed.

The enlightened one concluded this story saying, "The ascetic at that time was I who am today the fully enlightened one."

The moral: "A divinity, when controlled by lust for physical beauty, is of lower status than a virtuous person."
Also,
"Even the happiness of a divinity can be subject to uncontrolled lust for physical beauty."

29 It is mentioned elsewhere, in Buddhaghosa's commentary to the *Samiddhi Sutta* of the *Saṁyuttanikāya*, that the divine nymph was his wife in a previous life. For the *Samiddhi Sutta* of the *Saṁyttanikāya*, see 'The Devas: The 'Paradise' Suttas', I, 2, §10 as in C. A. F. Rhys Davids and Sūriyagoḍa Sumaṅgala Thera, *The Book of Kindred Sayings [Saṃyutta-Nikāya] or Grouped Suttas*, Part I, *Kindred Sayings with Verses [Sagāthā Vagga]*, [1917]: 14-18.

168

The Story of a Little Bird's Hiding Place
(*Sakuṇagghi-Jātaka*)

The enlightened one who became supreme among all human beings, as is the top gem on a crown, was living in Jetavanārāma. At one time, he wanted to admonish his disciples about searching for alms. "Oh monks, it is always good to search for alms in the same manner that one's forebears did. It is not good to go to inhospitable places in search of alms, because that is dangerous." Saying so, he delivered the *Sakuṇa Sutta*, which appears in the *Mahāvagga* [of the *Saṁyuttanikāya*] in detail.[30] He repeated again, "Oh monks, oh monks, even birds when going in search of food were faced with disaster." And the monks requested the Buddha to disclose the former story.

At one time, King Brahmadatta was ruling the city of Benares. At that time, the Enlightenment Being was born as a small bird living in a field. She lived by eating things from under clods of ploughed up turf. She dwelt there with her family. One time she thought she would go to a different habitat to find food, and she went to a certain flat land. There she searched for food. In the meantime, a certain falcon swooped down without being noticed and plucked up the small bird. The small bird, while she was being carried by the falcon, started to cry and said, "I came to an unsuitable habitat to search for food, and because of that I have fallen into this situation. If I was in my own habitat, I would have known what to do." On hearing these words of the little bird, the falcon said, "If

30 See the *Sakuṇovāda Sutta* in the *Saṁyuttanikāya*, *Mahāvagga*, 'Kindred Sayings on the Stations (or Arisings) of Mindfulness: Ambapālī', III, I, vi, as in F. L. Woodward, *The Book of the Kindred Sayings (Saṁyutta-Nikāya) or Grouped Suttas*, Part V (*Mahā-Vagga)*, 1930: 125-26. The name of this Sutta is given in the Udāna of the *Saṁyuttanikāya* as the *Sakuṇagghi Sutta*.

that is so, I will let you go to your own habitat. Stay there, and see if I am not able to catch you even there." Saying so, he dropped the little bird. Then the little bird, dropped in its habitat, stood on top of a clod of earth and said, "Now, try and see if you can catch me." Hearing her words, the falcon swooped down very fast to try to catch the little bird. When the falcon came very near, the little bird went underneath the ploughed up clod of earth, and hid. The falcon, which was swooping down very fast, could not control his speed and hit the ground hard with his chest. He died with his eyes looking up toward the sky.

The enlightened one, who was pointing out this story, said, "Oh monks, just as this small bird that went out from the place where her forebears searched for food came to trouble, in the same way, do not go to search for alms where your parent did not go because the same sort of thing will happen to you. Who is the parent of monks? He is the omnipresent Buddha. It is noble to follow the way he teaches. Just as the small bird went out from her own habitat and was seized by the falcon, in the same way you also will fall into trouble created by Māra[31] if you go where there is a beautiful woman without your controlling the five sensual faculties, such as your eyes, and so forth. Therefore, try to understand that by falling into the enslavement of the cravings of the five faculties, you will die before you reach enlightenment and will not be able to conquer Saṁsāra [the ocean of rebecoming]. Crossing over Saṁsāra is like the little bird's coming into her own habitat and there being free from the grasping of the falcon. Just as coming to her own habitat on being let loose by the falcon, you have come to my habitat. By so coming, you have overcome the power of Māra, the enemy." Saying so, the Buddha ended this story, which caused many people to attain the stream entrance state of mind [*sotāpatti*].

"Devadatta was the falcon at that time. And the little bird was I who am the fully enlightened one."

The moral: "Those who leave the Dhamma [the law] will fall into trouble."

31 Māra is Death, the Evil One.

169

The Story of Araka

(*Araka-Jātaka*)

Again, the Buddha who was like a lion to his Sakyā kin, when he was living in the Jeta Grove temple delivered this Jātaka story in order to emphasize 'The Discourse of Loving Kindness'.[32] This is how it was. The Buddha said:

Oh monks, one who develops loving kindness in his mind, and who practices loving kindness, will gain eleven worthwhile benefits. What are they? (1) He will sleep well. (2) He wakes up rested. (3) He does not have bad dreams. (4) He is loved by everyone. (5) He is pleasant even to demons. (6) He is loved by the gods. (7) He receives no harm from weapons, poison, fire, or other dangers, such as accidents. (8) His mind will be able to concentrate readily. (9) His look will be attractive. (10) When it is his time to die, he will die with a clear mind. (11) If he cannot gain a higher mental state in this life, after death he will be reborn in the Brahma world.

In this way, the Buddha explained the advantages of the constant practice of loving kindness.

Then, addressing the monks further, he added:

It is good to spread loving kindness to all living beings. And when one sees people who are suffering, one should be compassionate toward them. When one sees happy living beings, one should experience sympathetic joy. Toward all living beings, one should maintain the same attitude, behaving toward them with equanimity. These four sublime states of mind [*brahmavihāra*] ought to be observed by everyone constantly.

He preached to the monks in this way.

---

32 The *Metta Sutta*, or 'The Discourse of Loving Kindness', is in the *Suttanipāta*, verses 143-52 [=I.8.1-10].

Further, he extended his sermon saying, "Oh monks, even in the past noble people, developing loving kindness in their minds, after death in this life did not leave the Brahma world for seven births and seven deaths."

Then the monks invited the Buddha, with respect and honor, to disclose that story. The Buddha thereupon delivered the story of the past. This is how it was:

At one time, in a certain aeon, the Enlightenment Being was born in a Brahmin family and received a good education. He saw the disadvantages of the five sensual desires [*pañcakāma*-s]. Reflecting on this, he renounced the world and ordained himself as a Ṛṣi [an ascetic].[33] After his ordination, he obtained many followers and became their leader under the name of Araka. He became a very well-known teacher. He used to meditate on loving kindness, compassion, sympathetic joy, and equanimity. At such a time as he was practicing such meditation on the four sublime states of mind, he advised his followers to practice thus:

"Oh ascetics, if you are truly ascetics, you must spread loving kindness constantly in all the four directions and the four intermediate directions, as well as up and down, which together are known as the ten directions. In all those directions, whatsoever living beings there may be, will have all defilements removed from their minds by the power of your loving kindness."

Giving them this advice, he persuaded them to practice all the four sublime states of mind, and in this way to develop their minds.

Following the teacher's advice, they all developed their minds through the same meditation. All of them, at the end of their life spans, were born in the Brahma world. After that, they all enjoyed the happiness of the Brahma world for seven births, one after another, lasting seven aeons.

"The leader of the ascetics at that time called Araka was I who am today the Buddha."

The moral: "Foes of all types can be eliminated through loving kindness."

33 When there are the teachings of a Buddha in the world, people are ordained as Bhikkhu-s [monks]. At a time when there are no Buddha's teachings in the world, people can only ordain themselves as Ṛṣi-s.

170

The Story of a Chameleon [The Riddle of a Chameleon]

(*Kakaṇṭaka-Jātaka, Kakaṇṭaka-Pañha*)

This story will be found in the *Mahā-Ummagga-Jātaka* [No. 546]:

At one time, King Videha of the city of Mithilā went to walk in his pleasure garden with the four erudites and with Mahosadha. At that time, a certain chameleon was on the top of the archway at the entrance to the garden. When he saw that the king was coming toward him, he came down from his perch atop the archway and sat on the ground. The king saw the chameleon coming down from the archway and sitting on the ground to the side. He asked Mahosadha, "What is this chameleon doing?" Mahosadha said, "Your lordship, he is paying respect to you." The king responded, "It is not good to receive his service without giving something.[34] Let us give him something." Mahosadha, the Enlightenment Being, said, "Your lordship, it is useless for us to give him something valuable. Give him something to eat." The king asked, "What does he eat?" "Your lordship, he eats only meat."[35] The king asked, "How much worth of meat should we give?" Mahosadha said, "Give him meat equal in weight to one-and-a-half grains of rice." Then the king ordered one of his servants to give to the chameleon daily meat equal in weight to two-and-a-half grains of rice. The servant from that time used to daily give the chameleon that amount of meat, without fail.

On a certain full moon observance day, according to the king's order, no living beings were supposed to be killed. That day the servant searched

34 The chameleon has been acting as a servant, keeping a lookout over the garden for flies, spiders, and so forth, which are his preys.

35 Flies and spiders are considered to be meat.

throughout the whole city, but could not get any meat. Therefore, the servant took a little piece of gold and made a hole in its center through which he put a string, and he made it as if it were a necklace. Because of this, the chameleon became conceited.

The next day, the king went again to walk in the pleasure garden with the four erudites and Mahosadha. On that day, the chameleon did not come down to the side of the road as before, but stayed atop the archway. The king saw this, and asked Mahosadha why the chameleon was not coming down to the side of the road as before. Mahosadha determined the reason for this through his power of thought. He observed that the chameleon was now wearing the necklace. He disclosed to the king that the reason was the chameleon's conceit on account of its having been given the necklace. Then, on hearing this, the king summoned the servant and questioned him as to why he gave the chameleon the piece of gold strung as a necklace. The servant explained why he did so. Then the king understood the chameleon's conceit. And he was surprised how Mahosadha had understood this immediately. He appreciated Mahosadha's wisdom and understanding even more.

The moral: "Wealth easily brings conceit."

171

The Story of an Auspicious State
(*Kalyāṇadhamma-Jātaka*)

Buddha, who was most prominent among the Sakyā kin, was living in Jetavanārāma. While he was there, one pious layman who always used to visit him came one evening with flowers, perfumes, and lights in his spread open hands to listen to the Dhamma.

While he was away from home, his wife's mother came to his home and asked her daughter, "Does your husband live happily with you?" Hearing this, she said, "Oh mom, my husband is like a pious monk. He lives happily." The mother was a little hard of hearing, and she heard, "My husband has gone to become a monk." On hearing these words, she quickly started to cry. Those who were nearby, all the family members, servants, and retinue, hearing the sound of her crying, also started to cry loudly. Hearing their noise, neighbors came into the house and they inquired as to the reason for the crying. They heard the news that the pious householder had gone to become a monk.

At that time, the pious householder who was returning home from the temple came to his street. A neighbor, who was at that same time leaving home to visit the Buddha, met him on his way. He said to the pious man, "At your home there is a big hullabaloo. People at your home are crying, saying that you have gone to become a monk." The pious man thought, on hearing these words, "It is not good to do harm to the good name that has come to me." And he returned to Jetavanārāma where monks were living. He met the Buddha there. The Buddha asked, "Oh pious layman, you just now left the temple. Why have you returned?" He said, "Your reverence, even without being ordained as a monk, I have heard from someone that I have been ordained. Thinking that I should not give up the good name that has fallen to me, I have come to be ordained." The Buddha, hearing this, said, "That is good," and he gave him ordination. Within a few days, after meditation, he developed his insight and attained Arahant-ship.

One day, the monks gathered in the preaching hall were talking to each other until the Buddha came there. They said, "Such-and-such a pious householder, thinking not to destroy the good name that had come to him, became ordained. Immediately after ordination, he attained sainthood, destroying all his defilements." Meanwhile the Buddha came there and asked, "Oh monks, what were you talking about before I came?" The monks then mentioned about what they had been talking.

Hearing this, the Buddha said, "Oh monks, even in the past noble people like him did not give up their good name when such came to them." The monks asked the Buddha to disclose how it was. The Buddha then related the story of old:

At one time, there was a king called Brahmadatta ruling in Benares. At that time, the Enlightenment Being was born to the home of the city's millionaire. After he grew up, the millionaire died. Taking his place, he used to go to perform service for the king every day. One time, just as in the present story, a similar incident took place. The millionaire's family started to cry loudly at home.

At the same time, the millionaire, who was the Enlightenment Being, was coming home from performing service in the palace. He heard from someone who was on the road that his home was in an uproar, with people saying that he had gone to become an ascetic. He, thinking not to destroy the good name that had come to him, returned to the king's palace. The king saw him and asked, "You just left from performing service here. Why are you suddenly back?" He said, "Your lordship, I would like to be ordained as an ascetic. Since a good name has come to me while a layman, it would not be good to destroy such a good name while I have it. As a living being who has shame and fear of doing unwholesome deeds, it is my responsibility to maintain and protect my credibility. Therefore, I will maintain and protect the good name that has come to me. So, your lordship, I wish to be ordained and to practice asceticism. I have no craving for the enjoyment of the five sensual desires."[36] Saying so, he got permission from the king to become an ascetic. He went to the Himalayan forest, and there he became an ascetic. He meditated and gained the five higher knowledges [*pañcābhiññā*][37] and the eight mental absorptions [*jhāna*-s].[38] Without losing those states of mental absorption, he lived his lifetime. After that, he was born among the Brahma deities.

Buddha ended this Jātaka story of an auspicious state in this way:

"The king of Benares at that time is today the Venerable elder Ānanda. The ascetic [the millionaire of Benares] is today I who am the Buddha, the fully enlightened one."

The moral: "Protecting a good name one acquires, no matter how, aids one in obtaining a higher status."

36 For the five sensual desires, see note 25 above.

37 For the five higher knowledges, see note 20 above.

38 For the eight mental absorptions, see note 21 above with regard to the eightfold concentrations.

172

The Story of a Noisy Sound
(*Daddara-Jātaka*)

When the enlightened one who became the noblest of the Sakyā kin was living in Jetavanārāma in Sāvatthi, this story was delivered with regard to the elder Kokālika.

In the city of Sāvatthi, in various places, monks were learning by heart the Buddha's preachings. At that time, the elder Kokālika heard that other monks were preaching, and he could not preach. But he wanted to hide his shortcoming. And for the sake of hiding his weakness, he said, "I also know how to preach. If there are monks to listen, then I can preach." He went from place to place saying so.

Hearing this, the monks said, "Venerable Kokālika, if it is so, today you can preach." And he accepted. Then the monks prepared good food and gruel, as well as sweets, to venerate and pay respect to him. Having enjoyed the food, adorned with a very bright yellow robe and underskirt, he set about to preach. He started inviting others to listen to the Dhamma saying, "Meritorious people, this is the time to listen to the Dhamma [*Dhammassavanakālo ayaṁ, bhadantā*]." In this way, he summoned many monks to the preaching hall, and they sat down around him. First he paid respect to the elderly monks. Then he took a beautiful fan, went toward the pulpit, and sat down there. He started to preach. When he recited one line out of the first stanza of the preaching, he forgot the other lines. And he became silent. From his whole body, he started to perspire. The perspiration soaked his body, and he became very afraid and ashamed, as he could not preach as he said he could. He descended from the pulpit, and bending his head downwards, he fled away. At that time, another monk who was capable went up to the pulpit and preached, satisfying the monks in the audience.

One day, those elders who assembled in the preaching hall said, "We thought that elder Kokālika would be able to preach. But now we understand that he knows nothing, and is incapable of preaching." In the meantime, the Buddha visited that place and asked, "Oh monks, what were you talking about before I came here?" On hearing what they were talking about, the omnipresent one disclosed a previous story about the elder Kokālika:

At one time, in the city of Benares when King Brahmadatta was ruling, the Enlightenment Being was born as a lion who lived in a cave in the forest. Near the cave, there lived also a jackal. One day, there was a lot of rain. Afterward, many lions came near to the Enlightenment Being's cave and roaring, they played. On seeing this, the jackal also came out and started to play, howling. When the lions heard the howling, they became silent.

There was a lion cub that was the son of the lion who was the Enlightenment Being. He asked, "Revered father, why did all the lions stop playing all at once?" The lion king said, "Even though we are animals, we are born in high status. While we were playing, that menial jackal[39] came to play at the same time, comparing himself to us. Therefore, we were ashamed to play, so we stopped."

The enlightened one then concluded this Jātaka story about a noisy sound [the jackal's howling]:

"The elder Kokālika was at that time the jackal. The Venerable Rāhula [the Buddha Gotama's son] was the lion cub. The lion king was I who am today the Buddha."

The moral: "Small people just make a big sound."

39 Lions kill animals when they get hungry, and they eat. Jackals, without making any effort, eat the leftovers from the lions. Therefore, they are menial.

173

The Story of a Monkey
(*Makkaṭa-Jātaka*)

When the Buddha, the fully enlightened one, was living in Jeta Grove monastery, this story was disclosed with regard to a monk who was devious in a deceitful and hypocritical way.

The present story here appears in the *Udāla-Jātaka* [No. 487] in detail, in the *Pakiṇṇaka* [=the fourteenth book of the *Jātaka*].

[There was a certain monk who was practicing the ways of gainfulness in a hypocritical fashion. One day, the monks in the preaching hall were discussing his wrong ways of being a monk. While they were discussing this, the Buddha visited there. The Buddha asked them what they were discussing before his arrival. Then the monks told him what they were discussing, and mentioned the hypocritical nature of the monk.]

Here, the Buddha said, "Oh monks, this monk in his previous life also in a devious way tried to warm himself by a fire." The monks thereupon requested the Buddha to disclose the story. The Buddha disclosed it this way:

At one time, when King Brahmadatta was ruling in Benares, the Enlightenment Being was born as a householder. At that time, his wife gave birth to a son. While the son was growing up, his wife died. Then the Enlightenment Being, with his son, renounced lay life, leaving behind all his wealth while his relatives were crying. He went to the Himalayan forest, made a hermitage, and lived there with his son.

One day there came a great deal of rain. The Enlightenment Being was lying on his bed at that time, while his son was massaging his feet.

In the meantime, a certain monkey who was feeling cold thought, "If I go to the hermitage, the hermits will not let me in. Therefore, let me disguise myself as a hermit, and then they will let me in." Thinking so, he put on a dead ascetic's bark garment and sat down under a Palmyra palm tree in front of the hermitage. The Enlightenment Being's son went out for a short while and saw the monkey sitting there. He thought that he was another ascetic. Thinking so, he went inside to his father and told him that there was another ascetic outside, and it would be good if they could invite him into their hut to warm himself by the fire.

The father ascetic got up from his bed, came outside, and saw the monkey sitting in front of the hermitage. He said to his son, "Oh my son, an ascetic has no such a face. He must be a monkey. If he comes in to enjoy the warmth of the fire, no doubt he will burn down the hermitage."[40] He took a hot brand, and threw it toward the monkey. The monkey left behind the bark garment, and climbed up into a tree.

The Enlightenment Being, cultivating the meditation of the four sublime states of mind,[41] gained mental absorption. At the end of his life, without falling down from his mental absorption, he was after his death born in the Brahma world.

"The monkey at that time was the monk who practiced a deceitful way of life. The Enlightenment Being's son was the Venerable Rāhula [the Buddha Gotama's son]. And I, the Buddha, who has attained enlightenment, was the ascetic." Saying so, the Buddha ended this story.

The moral: "Ends cannot be obtained through trickery."

40 This is because monkeys are foolish.
41 For the four sublime states of mind, see note 26 above.

174

The Story of a Treacherous Monkey [The Second Story of a Monkey]

(*Dūbhiyamakkaṭa-Jātaka, Dutiya-Makkaṭa-Jātaka*)

While the fully enlightened one who was the top gem of the Sakyā kin was living at the Bamboo Grove temple, this story was spoken about Devadatta.

One day the monks who were assembled in the preaching hall were talking about the monk named Devadatta who was ungrateful and of a treacherous nature, and who did not even understand the meaning of gratitude. While they were talking about this, the fully enlightened one, the Buddha, visited there and asked the monks, "What were you talking about before I came?" The monks said, "Your lordship, we were not talking about anything other than the ungrateful and treacherous nature of Devadatta." The Buddha said, "Oh monks, it is not only now that Devadatta is ungrateful and treacherous. He was so even before." Then the monks invited the Buddha to disclose the former story of the lack of gratitude and treachery of Devadatta.

At one time when Benares was ruled by King Brahmadatta, the Enlightenment Being was born in a Brahmin family in the state of Benares. Later, he renounced the enjoyment of the five sensual desires,[42] and he became an ascetic.

While he was practicing asceticism, there was a severe drought. One day, while he was walking on a road, he saw that many birds could not get water to drink. When people were walking on the road, they were given water. But when there were no people on the road, they could not get

42 For the five sensual desires, see note 25 above.

any. At that time, people did not go to that area for a considerable period of time. Because of this, many birds had no water to quench their thirst.

At that same time, a monkey was waiting near a certain well for someone to draw water for the benefit of living beings. While he was waiting, the Enlightenment Being was passing through that village. He saw the thirsty monkey and realized that he was waiting for water. Considering the sad plight of living beings, the Enlightenment Being drew water from the well and drank and washed himself. He then set out some water to drink for the sake of living beings. The monkey came and drank water as much as he wanted. He filled up his stomach until he was satisfied. After he had finished drinking, he ran up a tree and began to mock the Enlightenment Being. Seeing that, the Enlightenment Being said, "Is this good? I have given water to such an ungrateful person as you who, without being grateful, mocks me. You do not know how to be grateful." Hearing these words, the monkey said, "There is no such thing as gratitude for us monkeys. I will even do something else to you." Saying this, he dropped his feces on the Enlightenment Being and ran away. The Enlightenment Being thought, "Menial living beings do such menial things to good people." Thinking so, he cleansed himself again and without giving it a second thought, he did not get angry at the monkey whom he had treated with loving kindness and patience. And he continued on his way.

Saying this, the enlightened one completed this story of a monkey.

He then added, "At that time, Devadatta was the monkey. And I who have become the fully enlightened one was the ascetic who helped the monkey."

The moral: "Gratitude is a noble quality for everyone to develop."

175

The Story of a Sun-Worshipper
(*Ādiccupaṭṭhāna-Jātaka*)

At one time, when the fully enlightened one was living in Jetavanārāma, this story was delivered about a monk who was known to be a trickster.

The monk who was a trickster was taken to the Buddha for admonition. The Buddha said, "Oh monk, not only today but even in the past you were a trickster and deceived others." The other monks then requested the Buddha to disclose how he was in the past. The Buddha, disclosing the past, said thus:

At one time, King Brahmadatta was ruling the city of Benares. At that time, the Enlightenment Being was born in the village called Kāsigāma in a Brahmin family. When he came of age, he left his home and renounced attachment to the five sensual desires.[43] He became a solitary ascetic observing all precepts and living in the Himalayan Mountains. Later, he became the leader of many ascetics who had come to study under him.

Once during the time of the spring retreat, all those ascetics left the forest and went to a village in search of sizeable provisions of salt and sours. The villagers, on seeing these serene ascetics, requested that they stay there and made a hermitage for them. The ascetics accepted this hermitage, and lived there.

At that time, when the ascetics left their hermitage on their daily alms round, a monkey used to come to their hermitage and, getting in, would spill the water containers, turn over all the pots, and leave droppings all about.

43 For the five sensual desires, see note 25 above.

The ascetics lived there during the three months of the spring retreat. At its end, they said to the villagers, "Devotees, we are leaving tomorrow." The devotees said, "Venerable sirs, we are preparing lunch for tomorrow. Please accept it from us, and afterwards you may leave." The ascetics agreed to this.

The next day, the devotees made various types of delicacies and took them to the hermitage where the ascetics lived. On seeing them come, the monkey thought, "If I appeared as serene as these ascetics, I also might be able to get these delicacies." Positioning himself in a certain pose, he sat gazing at the sun pretending to be a serene and silent person. The devotees who brought food for the ascetics saw the monkey who was sitting like an ascetic. Seeing his posture and silent demeanor, the devotees said, "Look, when someone associates with serene people, they also become serene." Saying so, they expressed their appreciation of the monkey's behavior. The ascetics said, "Devotees, this monkey has no good qualities. Why do you express appreciation of his behavior? If you must know his nature, when we go to the village for our alms round, he spoils all the hermitage leaving his droppings everywhere, he breaks our water pots, and he does other major damage to the hermitage." In this way, they explained what the monkey used to do.

On hearing this, the devotees took sticks and rocks, and chased away the monkey. The ascetics then went back to the Himalayan forest and practiced strict asceticism. They were eventually born in the Brahma world.

Saying so, the fully enlightened one completed this story of a sun-worshipper.

"The monkey at that time was born today as this trickster monk. The ascetics are today the followers of the Buddha. And the leader of the ascetics is today myself, the fully enlightened one."

The moral: "Tricksters are always looked down upon by everyone."

176

The Story of a Fist of Chickpeas
(*Kalāyamuṭṭhi-Jātaka*)

When the omnipresent one was living in Jeta Grove temple, this story was told about the king of Kosala.

At that time, peasants in a remote village were fearful of an enemy king who was about to attack them. On hearing this news the king of Kosala, setting out, approached Jetavanārāma with his army just before the rainy season and set up an encampment there. When there the king thought, "I am setting forth in an unseasonable time. Therefore, I will see the Buddha, the omnipresent one, and he will ask me, 'Oh king, where are you going?' I will tell the Buddha that I am going to wage a war. The Buddha, who not only advises me for the betterment of my mind for the future world, will be able to see the future. And he will be able to predict whether or not it is good to go at this time. If it is good to go, he will keep silent." Thinking so, he went to see the Buddha.

The omnipresent one, seeing the king, asked, "Your lordship, where are you going on this mid-day?" The king of Kosala said, "Your Venerable lordship, I am going to destroy a group of enemies in a remote village. Before going, I am coming to see you and to pay my respects to you, the Buddha." On hearing this from the king, the all-knowing lord said, "Your lordship, it is not good to go at this unseasonable springtime." He then said further, "Even in the past, a certain king, on hearing a noble one's advice, stopped his foray to war." The king then asked how it was, and invited the omnipresent one to disclose the ancient story. The story was disclosed in this way:

At one time, Benares was ruled by King Brahmadatta. While he was ruling, the Enlightenment Being was advising the king in all his royal activities. At that time, there was a riot against the king in a remote region. Then the king left the capital and came to the pleasure garden with his army. He there organized the attack, staying there for two or three days. While the army was staying there, one day servants brought hot food for the horses and put it in a large trough to cool off. A stray monkey then happened by, and he took in his hand and mouth some of the chickpeas, and ran up a tree. Sitting on a branch of the tree, he was eating. One chickpea fell down. Suddenly, he forgot everything, he put down all the other chickpeas, and he came down the tree and started to search for it. He could not find it. Then he climbed up the tree and sat there, being very melancholy as if he were a person who had lost a thousand gold coins.

The king asked the Enlightenment Being, pointing towards the monkey, "Sir, did you see what that monkey has just done?" The Enlightenment Being said, "Yes, I noticed. That monkey, for the sake of a single chickpea, left aside all his food. In the same way, for the sake of a little thing of value, it is not good to leave aside something large of large value. In this unseasonable time, if you go forward to war with such a big army, it will be similar to the monkey who left a large quantity of food for the sake of one chickpea." And the king then turned back, stopping his foray into battle.

Hearing the words of the omnipresent one, the king of Kosala also halted his foray into battle and returned to his own city. And the Buddha ended this story of *Kalāyamuṭṭhi-Jātaka* [this 'Story of a Fist of Chickpeas'].

"King Brahmadatta at that time is today the Venerable Ānanda. And the minister was I, who today has become the Buddha."

The moral: "It is foolishness to leave aside much for the sake of a small benefit."

177

The Story of a Velvet Apple Tree
(*Tiṇḍuka-Jātaka*)

When the fully enlightened one who became the eye of the Sakyā kin[44] was living in the Jeta Grove temple, this story was disclosed to explain the Buddha's intellectuality, his perfection of wisdom.

In the same way that the *Mahābodhi-Jātaka* [No. 528] and the *Ummagga-Jātaka* [No. 546] explain the perfection of wisdom, this Jātaka also explains the Buddha's wisdom.

When the monks were assembled in the preaching hall at the time of the Buddha's evening Dhamma sermon, the Buddha entered and asked, "Oh monks, what were you talking about before I came here?" Then the monks said, "Your Venerable lordship, we were talking about your wisdom." The Buddha said, "Oh monks, not only now, even when I was born as an animal, I was able to save many living beings from danger through the help of my past wisdom." The monks asked the Buddha to disclose the story of the past. And the Buddha disclosed the story in this way:

At one time, Benares was ruled by a king called Brahmadatta. At that time, the Enlightenment Being was born as the leader of a troop of 80,000 monkeys living in the Himalayan Mountains. They used to come, from time to time, from the forest to a village, around which they encamped. There was in the middle of the village a very big velvet apple tree that was endowed with a great quantity of both fruit and leaves. When the people would leave the village to go into the forest for work, the monkeys would come into the village and would eat the fruit. When the people returned, the monkeys left for the forest.

---

44 Just as the eye is the most worthy of all the faculties, so the Buddha was the most worthy of all the Sakyā-s.

Now, the people in the village built their houses with bamboo, thatching the houses with bamboo leaves, and latching their doors with bamboo latches. The velvet apple tree in the village was at one time full of fruit with its branches weighed down with the weight of the fruit and touching the ground. The monkeys at the same time were wondering whether or not there was fruit on the tree. Without their all going there, they sent a monkey spy. The monkey spy went alone, saw that the tree was well laden with fruit, and came back to the head monkey reporting this. Hearing this, all the monkeys suggested that they go there. But the head monkey asked whether or not there were humans in the village. He said, "If there are people there, it is not good to go there to get the fruit of the velvet apple tree." Even though he said this, all the other monkeys came together and said, "But your lordship, let us hide around the village in the daytime. And let us go in the middle of the night into the village to eat the velvet apples. In this way, we can come back safely after eating the fruit."

Saying such things to the leader of the troop, they persuaded him that they should go in the middle of the night.

Near the village there was a large slab of stone. There they assembled until the middle of the night. In the middle of the night, they came into the village to the tree to eat. But a villager came out of his house to go to do his toilet in the middle of the night, and he saw the monkeys who were on the tree. He shouted, and informed the other villagers that there were many monkeys on the tree. People came out of their houses and surrounded the tree holding weapons, clubs, rocks, and so forth, and they prevented the monkeys from leaving. They were waiting until the morning to kill them all.

The monkeys, seeing all the people surrounding them, became very afraid. They thought, "There is no way for us to get out of this." And they came to the leader of the troop and begged him, "Your lordship, many people have surrounded the tree brandishing weapons, clubs, and so forth, without allowing us to leave. No doubt they are thinking of killing us in the morning. Please tell us a way to get out of this disaster."

The Enlightenment Being said, "Do not be afraid of this trouble. Human beings will flee when there is trouble elsewhere."

Telling them not to worry, he summoned a small monkey and asked him to go to a house where there was an old woman making cotton thread, and to take a firebrand and set the village on fire. The small monkey went to that place pretending to be a little child. He went to the fireplace, took a firebrand, and coming out of the house he set fire to the village.

Seeing the village burning, the people ran to quench the fire. And the monkeys came down from the tree and ran out of the village.

Meanwhile, the monkey called Senaka grabbed one velvet apple and ran.

Saying so, the Buddha ended this story of the *Tiṇḍuka-Jātaka* [this 'Story of a Velvet Apple Tree'].

"The young monkey Senaka, who was the nephew of the leader of the troop of monkeys at that time, is today the Sakyā noble Mahānāma. And the troop of monkeys are today the followers of the Buddha. I who have become the Buddha was at that time the king of the monkeys."

The moral: "Learn to think wisely to be able to overcome all disasters."

178

The Story of a Tortoise
(*Kacchapa-Jātaka*)

While the omnipresent one who became the characterizing mark [*tilaka*] of the Sakyā kin was living in Jeta Grove temple, this Jātaka story regarding plague[45] was disclosed.

In the city of Sāvatthi, in a millionaire's family, there arose plague. When that disease arose in their home everything was dying, including dogs, chickens, and so forth. At that time, the millionaire addressed his son, saying, "Son, make a hole in the wall and leave home through it.[46] If you leave like that, then you will be able to recover from the disease. So, run away from our home into the forest, and stay there until the disease is finished with.[47] When the disease is finished with, come back to this place and dig up the wealth that I have hidden where I will show you. Take that wealth and leave this place. With it, start a new life elsewhere marrying a suitable girl and having a family." The millionaire's son agreed to run away like this.

When that millionaire's son agreed to do this, making a hole in the wall and running away, on his way he saw the Buddha. The Buddha asked him, "From where did you come?" He said, "Such-and-such is my home. Plague has arisen there. So I fled away, saving my life, and leaving behind my relatives."

---

45 *ahivātakaroga*, a deadly infectious disease, plague. It is said that it can be caught from the smell of the venom of a cobra.

46 Going through a hole in the wall, instead of the door, is a way of outsmarting the spirit of disease and its power to chase after you.

47 For reasons of ritual purity after people die, this means that he would have to stay in the forest for 6 months.

The omnipresent one, listening to him, said, "It is good that you have done so. Not only today, but also in the past, some people seeing disaster arising somewhere, have left that place and they survived. Those who were attached to their homes, thinking, 'This place is my dwelling. How can I leave it?', they perished."

On hearing that, the millionaire's son said, "How was it before, sir? Kindly disclose it to me." And the omnipresent one disclosed the ancient story:

At one time when Brahmadatta was ruling the city of Benares, the Enlightenment Being was born as a potter who supported his family by making pots.

At that time, near the Ganges River at Benares, there was a little pond. This pond, when there was a lot of rain, joined with the Ganges. When fish, tortoises, and other aquatic animals knew by instinct that there would be a drought in a certain year, they swam into the Ganges. When they understood that there would be rain in the next year, they stayed in the pond. One year, they understood there would be no rain in the next year, so they fled the pond. One tortoise, though, thought, "My parents lived here. I, too, have grown up here. So, it is not good to leave this place." And he decided to stay there. With such thought, he determined not to leave the place, being attached to it. In the course of time, the drought came and little by little, water disappeared in the pond. And the pond became just mud and clay.

At this time, the Enlightenment Being went to that lake to get clay for making pots. The tortoise, at the same time, was moving in the mud and clay in the same spot. The Enlightenment Being, the potter, dug for clay in that spot and hit the head of the tortoise. On seeing him, the potter pulled him out and placed him on the ground, thinking that he was a large lump of clay. Then the tortoise said, with pain, "Oh potter, who has been born to a family of potters, it is not good to crave a place thinking, 'This is the place where I was born.'" Saying this advice, he died.

The potter, who was a wise person, thought he would give this message to the villagers. He took the tortoise in his arms, went to the nearby village, and said, "Look! This tortoise did not give up his birthplace even when he saw all his relatives leave. Because of this, he perished. He advised me, saying two stanzas, not to crave living pleasures with the thoughts, 'This is my birthplace. This is my relatives' place. This is my place of comfort. These are my children. This is my wife. These are my relatives. These are my possessions. This is my wealth. These are my reapings.' Thinking so, if you crave the place where you live, you will face disaster, just as this tortoise died with pain." And he admonished the people not to crave, as if he were a Buddha.

This admonition was spread throughout the 10,000 Yojana-s of Jambudīpa.[48] The potter's admonition, given at that time, was remembered in Jambudīpa for 7,000 years.

Saying this, the Buddha, the fully enlightened one, ended this Jātaka story of a tortoise.

"The tortoise at that time is today the Venerable Ānanda. And the potter at that time was I who am today the Buddha."

The moral: "Holding on tightly with craving to familiar things, such as the sensual desires, leads to disaster."

48 1 *Yojana* = roughly 7 miles. Jambudīpa is India of the Buddha's time.

179

The Story of Satadhamma (perhaps, Sattadhamma) [One with a Hundred Natures (or, with Seven Natures)]

(*Satadhamma-Jātaka, Sattadhamma-Jātaka*)

The Buddha, who was born to his Sakyā kin as a pot that gives the world all wishes, delivered this Jātaka story on account of monks gaining the fourfold requisites of a monk by the 21 unlawful means.

At one time, many monks used to earn their livelihood by doing wrongful services that monks were not supposed to do, such as being physicians, or running messages from people who were ploughing or sowing grain in the fields, or other of the 21 activities that were not accepted by the Buddha for monks to do for the sake of earning robes, food, shelter, and medicine [the fourfold requisites of a monk].

When the Buddha heard this news, he thought about the results of that wrongful behavior that those monks would have to experience in their future births, such as being born as animals, hungry ghosts, demons, or being born in hell. On account of this, he summoned all the monks and said, "Oh monks, if you earn your livelihood by doing the 21 things that I have asked you not to do, it is like eating balls of molten iron, or like eating poison. It is like a high caste person eating the food left over by someone of low caste. And he narrated this story without any invitation to do so. He said, "Oh monks, a young Brahmin named Satadhamma ate leftover food, and because of this he committed suicide." And he narrated the following story:

At one time, there was a king called Brahmadatta ruling the city of Benares. The Enlightenment Being was born at that time in a low caste community [*caṇḍāla*]. At one point, he was going to a far-away village, carrying with him some cooked rice in a rolled-up leaf packet and a measurement of uncooked rice in a separate packet. At the same time, another man born in a high-class Brahmin family set forth on the same road without any provisions. On the way, the two met and the Brahmin asked the low caste man, "Who are you? In what community were you born?" The Enlightenment Being, who was not in the habit of lying, replied, "I am of a low caste community." He then asked, "Of what community are you?" The Brahmin said, "I am a high-class Brahmin, born in a long line of high-class Brahmins."

The low caste man said, "If that is so, can I travel together with you?" The high-class Brahmin agreed to this.

On the way, when they reached a lake where there was water to drink and in which to bathe, they went down to the lake and bathed. Then the low caste man, opening his packet of rice, before he had eaten any, asked the high-class Brahmin, "Will you accept some rice? Afterwards, I will eat." On hearing that, the Brahmin said, "Hey! Low caste fellow! Do you think that I would eat the rice that you, a low caste person, has brought?" And he refused. Then the low caste man ate half of his packet of cooked rice, and kept the leftovers for the evening meal.

They then started to walk again on their journey. All the day, they walked. In the evening, because they were so tired from walking, they became very hungry. They went to a nearby river. At the river, they took a break. The low caste man thought that as the Brahmin had refused to eat any of his rice in the afternoon, there was no need to ask him to eat again. And he started to eat.

When he started to eat, the Brahmin lost his mind because he was so hungry. Since he had not been offered any rice, he thought he would take some by force. And he grabbed some rice, eating these leftovers.[49] After eating, he went to the river and washed his fingers and mouth.

---

49 Because the low caste man had already started eating, the rice that the Brahmin grabbed was considered to be leftovers.

When he came back from the river, he began to regret what he had done, thinking, "Oh, what have I done! I have eaten the leftovers of a low caste man. And even so, this was not enough for me to eat. Further, since I was so crazed with hunger I took it by force, rather than beg it from him. Therefore, it was stolen by me. Having been born in a high-class Brahmin family, I have done a very bad deed that can bring disrepute to my family." Thinking this, he decided to kill himself. He then ran into the forest and committed suicide.

Buddha, the fully enlightened one, said, "Oh monks, the disciples of the Buddha are not supposed to make unlawful earnings that may cause regrets that they could not follow the Buddha's advice. It is not good to eat wrongfully, as was done by this Brahmin. It may cause you not to be able to escape the unending cycle of births and deaths [*saṁsāra*] and unending suffering as happened to the Brahmin Satadhamma."

Saying this, he ended the Jātaka story of Satadhamma.

"At that time, I who have become the fully enlightened one was the low caste man."

The moral: "One should act in accordance with one's nature."

(180)

The Story of a Difficult Giving [as when in adversity]

(*Duddada-Jātaka*)

When the Buddha, who became like a crown to the Sakyā kin, was living in Jeta Grove Temple, this story was delivered. Some of the Buddha's devotees had given a dutiful donation [*dāna*] to the monks. The monks requested that the Buddha disclose the story of old behind the donation.

At one time when King Brahmadatta was ruling in the city of Benares, the Enlightenment Being was born in a Brahmin family. When he was grown up, on seeing the disadvantages of the five sensual desires[50] and the advantage of becoming an ascetic, he ordained himself an ascetic. In the course of time, he gained many followers. They all lived in the Himalayan Mountains.

Once, when it was time for the spring retreat, they decided to go first to Benares and collect some salt and sours for their retreat. At that time one pious householder in the city of Benares, getting the support of many, gave donations of food to those ascetics for seven days. On the last day, the head of the group of pious householders said, "Venerable sirs, is it better to give a big donation than a small donation? What is the difference? Is the acquired merit the same?" The head of the ascetics said, "No matter whether a donation is small or big, giving is greatly appreciated by solitary Buddhas [*pacceka-buddha*-s] and their disciples [*arahant*-s]. Therefore, it is difficult to explain the fruit such as acquired merit. Even if you give a little thing as a donation, you will obtain the

50 For the five sensual desires, see note 25 above.

merit to be born in heaven and enjoy life there. If somebody thinks, 'What is the use of giving this trifling donation?' and so thinking, he does not give any donation, he has to suffer in woeful births."

Then, the ascetics were requested to stay in the city for the duration of the full four months of the rainy season.[51] They stayed there, and afterward they went back to the Himalayan forest. There they meditated on the four sublime states of mind,[52] and they gained mental absorption. After, they were born in the Brahma world without having lost their mental absorption.

Saying this, the Buddha finished disclosing this Jātaka story of a difficult giving [as when in adversity]:

"The ascetics at that time are today the followers of the Buddha. And their leader was I who am today the Buddha."

The moral: "No matter how little, it is good to give whenever you come across a person who needs charity."

51 That is, three months of the rainy season proper, and one month for receiving robes [*cīvaramāsa*].
52 For the four sublime states of mind, see note 26 above.

181

The Story of Asadisa [One without Comparison]

(*Asadisa-Jātaka*)

When the fully enlightened one who was like a hidden treasure belonging to the Sakyā kin was living in Jetavanārāma, he delivered this Jātaka story on his fulfillment of the perfection [*pāramī*, later *pāramitā*] of renunciation [*nekkhamma*].[53]

One day the monks who were assembled in the preaching hall in the evening, until the Buddha arrived, were discussing the Buddha's total renunciation of all worldly things. While they were talking about this, the Buddha came. The Buddha asked, "Oh monks, what were you talking about before I came?" The monks said, "Venerable sir, we were talking about your renunciation, which is without comparison." The Buddha said, "Oh monks, not only now when I, the omnipresent one, have become fully enlightened, but even before this birth in which I attained enlightenment I renounced a kingdom that came to me." Then the monks invited the Buddha to disclose how it was. The Buddha disclosed the story of old in this way:

At one time, the city of Benares was ruled by a king named Brahmadatta. The Enlightenment Being was born to that king's chief queen after nine-and-a-half months of pregnancy. At the time of the delivery of the baby, he was given the name, Prince Asadisa [One without Comparison].

53 There are ten perfections, the perfect exercise of the ten principle virtues of an Enlightenment Being, in Theravāda Buddhism. These are giving, or liberality [*dāna*], morality [*sīla*], renunciation [*nekkhamma*], wisdom [*paññā*], energy [*viriya*], patience [*khanti*], truthfulness [*sacca*], resolution [*adhiṭṭhāna*], loving kindness [*mettā*], and equanimity [*upekhā*].

After he had grown [some], another meritorious son was born. He was known as Prince Brahmadatta.

When Prince Asadisa was fully grown, he went to study at the university in Takkasilā. After he returned his father, who was about to die, summoned his ministers and said, "Ministers! When I die, the kingdom is to be ruled by Prince Asadisa. The viceroy [*uparājā*] should be Prince Brahmadatta." So ordering, he died.

After he passed away, the ministers wanted to invest Prince Asadisa with the crown. But on hearing this, Prince Asadisa refused to be king. So the ministers consecrated Prince Brahmadatta as king. They then wanted to name the Enlightenment Being, Prince Asadisa, viceroy. But this position also was not accepted by him. He wanted to remain just an ordinary prince, without any position.

Shortly, a certain minister of King Brahmadatta went to the king and said, "Your lordship, your brother wants to take the kingdom from you. He is trying to kill you." And he sowed suspicion in King Brahmadatta's mind about his brother. King Brahmadatta became upset, and he ordered Prince Asadisa to be seized.

The Enlightenment Being heard this news from a faithful minister, and he decided to flee the city of Benares. He went to a nearby king's city. He sent a message to that king that a clever archer had come to his city. The king then sent a messenger with a message that he would like to see him. When he arrived, Prince Asadisa questioned the king as to how much he would pay, requesting a hundred thousand gold coins a year. The king thought, "If he is such a clever archer, then I will be able to reduce the number of archers in my army." And the king agreed. After he had done so the remaining archers, since the new archer was paid more than them, became upset. They thought, "This man gets more than we get." Thinking so, they became jealous.

One day, the king went to his pleasure garden. He rested there under a mango tree. He requested that a bed be made for him there, and around it he had a curtain placed. While he was lying on the bed, he saw a cluster of mangoes high up on a top branch of the tree. He thought, "No one can reach these mangoes by climbing the tree. Let me send for my archers to shoot down the cluster of mangoes with their arrows." Thinking so, he summoned his archers. The archers came, and he requested them to bring down the cluster of mangoes with their arrows.

The archers said, "Your lordship, you have seen our skills. You have not yet seen the skills of the new archer who gets a hundred thousand gold coins as his annual stipend." The king then summoned the new archer, who was the Enlightenment Being. He ordered him to shoot down the cluster of mangoes. The new archer said, "Your lordship, I want to stand in the place where you are. Please order your bed to be moved." The other archers, seeing that he had no bow in his hand, said to one another, "Do not give him your bow." And they conspired in this way. The Enlightenment Being, once inside the curtain that had been placed around the king's bed, opened the bag he was carrying, took out a sword, and strapped it over his shoulder. He wrapped around his body a golden chain as a belt. He placed on his shoulders golden epaulets. Over one of his shoulders, he strapped a case filled with arrows. On his head, he put a golden turban. Taking out a folded-up bow, he opened it. Taking in his hand an arrow from the case, he came out from behind the curtain as if he were a young serpent deity. He asked, "Your lordship, shall I shoot down the cluster of mangoes with the arrow going up, or with the arrow coming down?"

The king said, "I have seen things shot down by an arrow going. I have never seen anything shot down by an arrow returning. Therefore, shoot it down with the arrow returning."

The Enlightenment Being then said, "Your lordship, my arrow will go up to the divine world called Cātummahārājika [The Heaven of the Four Kings].[54] Therefore, please wait for a few minutes, and then you will

---

54 This is the lowest of the divine worlds. It derives its name from the Four Great Kings who dwell there as guardians of the four cardinal directions, or quarters of the world.

see the results." Saying so, he shot up his arrow. That arrow, piercing the branch holding the mango cluster, went up into the sky and to the divine world. When the Enlightenment Being understood that it had reached the Cātummahārājika, he took another arrow into his hand and shot it at a faster speed. This hit the feather of the first arrow, which was then taken by the deities. The second arrow returned with the sound of thunder. Many people became surprised and frightened. They started to peer up into the sky to see what the noise was. The Enlightenment Being said, "Do not be alarmed. It is the arrow returning through the wind." When he said this, people became afraid of the arrow falling on them.

The arrow came down and hit the same place that the first arrow had pierced on going up. The Enlightenment Being in one hand caught the cluster of mangoes, and in the other caught the arrow. At the moment they saw this, the king's retinue cheered, whistling, snapping their fingers, and waving many kerchiefs, and they danced. And the king gave many valuable presents to the Enlightenment Being.

In the meantime, the absence of Prince Asadisa from the city of Benares was heard by seven [other] nearby kings, who then surrounded Benares and demanded that the city be surrendered to them, or they would take it by force. On hearing this, the king of Benares became very afraid. He asked for his brother, Prince Asadisa, and heard that he was in the service of [such-and-such] a nearby king. He summoned a minister, and said, "Go to my brother and tell him that I respect him, and in my stead kneel down and pay my respects to him. Ask him to return with you."

The minister went to see Prince Asadisa and did as he had been instructed. The Enlightenment Being, informing the king in whose service he was, got permission to take leave and came back to Benares. After coming to Benares, he went up to the city's citadel and wrote a message to the seven kings: "I am now in this city. This message I send to you with this arrow. Don't wait for a second arrow. If you do not go, I will kill you all with the second arrow." He shot his first arrow with the message attached, and it fell right on the plate from which the kings were eating. Since the arrow had been shot [with such skill] like that, the kings became very afraid of the second arrow. They fled, thinking, "No doubt, the second arrow will kill us."

The Enlightenment Being, without shedding even a drop of blood as small as a dewdrop, thus vanquished the seven kings.

Then King Brahmadatta came to see Prince Asadisa and said, "Respectable brother, the kingdom belongs to you. Even before I became king, it had been requested that you accept it. As you refused, I ruled the country. Now, too, you can rule the country."

On hearing this, Prince Asadisa said, "I give the kingdom to you. You rule the country righteously." And he again gave the kingdom to his brother to rule. He then renounced all royal enjoyments and retreated to the Himalayan forest. There he ordained himself as an ascetic, and meditated. By his meditation, he developed the five higher knowledges [*pañcābhiññā*][55] and the eightfold mental absorptions [*aṭṭhasamāpatti*],[56] and at the end of his life he was born in the Brahma world.

The Buddha, the fully enlightened one, addressing the monks, said, "Oh monks, that archer knew how to shoot so skillfully that he could split a horse's hair, or have his arrow go through even a small written character, intersect another moving arrow, or hit its mark just on the basis of his having heard the target's noise. Furthermore, he could shoot so forcefully that his arrow can go through a sandbag, or pierce a bale of hay and propel it forward together with the arrow in it. Furthermore, he could shoot so skillfully that his arrow can speed through the middle of a formation of horses and chariots without hitting anyone or anything, and so forcefully that his arrow can pierce through metal plates. This was one of the 64 arts[57] known by him. Even knowing such a number of arts,

55 For the five higher knowledges, see note 20 above.

56 For the eightfold mental absorptions, see note 21 above with regard to the eightfold concentrations.

57 For the 64 arts at which well cultured men and women in ancient India were supposed to be adept, see Vatsyāyana's *Kāmasūtra*, Part I, Chapter 3, as in

he renounced royal happiness and left the kingdom after removing his brother's fear.

Saying so, the fully enlightened one ended this Jātaka story of Asadisa.

"King Brahmadatta at that time is today the Venerable Ānanda. And I who have become the fully enlightened one was Asadisa."

The moral: "Wise and skillful people do not care about worldly pleasures."

any translation of this text, such as Alain Daniélou, *The Complete Kāma Sūtra, The First Unabridged Modern Translation of the Classic Indian Text by Vatsyāyana* ..., prepared with the help of Kenneth Hurry, 1994, which translation includes the commentaries; Wendy Doniger and Sudhir Kakar, *Kamasutra, A New Complete English Translation of the Sanskrit Text* ..., 2002; any of the many printings of Sir Richard Burton and F. F. Arbuthnot's classic 1883 translation; or others, such as S. C. Upadhyaya's 1963 translation.

182

The Story about Fighting a War
(*Saṅgāmāvacara-Jātaka*)

When the omnipresent one who became a wish-conferring tree was living in Jetavanārāma, he disclosed this Jātaka story on account of the Venerable Nanda.[58]

On the day that the Venerable Nanda became ordained his bride-to-be, Janapadakalyāṇī,[59] looking out her window, saw the Venerable Nanda leaving and called out to him, "Nanda, come back soon!" Later, recalling these words, he regretted again and again his monkhood. He became very unhappy about his ordination. And he became inconsolable and despondent.

When the omnipresent one learned of this through his divine mind, he went to Nanda's chamber. The Venerable Nanda made a seat for the omnipresent one, and the omnipresent one sat down. The omnipresent one asked, "Nanda, are you not happy with your ordination?" Nanda responded, "Revered sir, I am still attached to Janapadakalyāṇī. Therefore, I have no satisfaction with my ordination." In this way, he disclosed his plight.

The Buddha said, "Nanda, have you ever been to the Himalayan forest?" Nanda said, "No, revered sir, I have never been there." The Buddha said, "If that is so, let us go visit there." The Venerable Nanda said, "How can I go without miraculous powers?" The Buddha said, "You can go with my miraculous powers." Nanda agreed.

Holding the Venerable Nanda's hand, the Buddha went up into the sky with him. On the way the Buddha, by his psychic powers, made

---

58 Nanda was the Buddha's half-brother, his stepmother's son by his father.

59 This is a title signifying that she was at that time the most beautiful young girl in the state.

appear a burnt forest. In it, on a burnt stump of a tree, there was sitting a certain she-monkey whose tail, ears, and nose were burnt. Pointing her out to him, the Buddha said, "Nanda, did you see that she-monkey?" Nanda said, "Yes, sir." The Buddha said, "Remember this she-monkey, Nanda." They then continued to the Himalayan forest.

Once in the Himalayan forest, the Buddha showed Nanda the four great lakes[60] and the five rivers,[61] magnificent mountains, and many other beautiful places. He asked, "Have you ever seen the divine world known as Cātummahārājika?"[62] The Venerable Nanda said, "No, I have never seen it." Then the Buddha said, "If that is so, then let us go there and see it." Saying so, the Buddha went to the divine abode known as Cātummahārājika and sat on the seat called Paṇḍukambalasīlāsana belonging to Sakka, the king of divine beings.[63]

Sakka, the king of the gods, heard that the Buddha had come to his divine world and, followed by divine beings and nymphs, he came to see the Buddha. Sakka sat down on one side of the Buddha[64] with 500 nymphs to his side. Those nymphs, who were very beautiful and had feet the complexion of doves, also came to see the Buddha. Buddha asked the Venerable Nanda, "Nanda, what do you think? Who is more beautiful, Janapadakalyāṇī or these nymphs?" Then the Venerable Nanda said, "Your reverence, compared to these nymphs, Janapadakalyāṇī is like that she-monkey we saw earlier in the burnt forest." When Nanda said this, Janapadakalyāṇī was no longer attractive to him since he had seen

---

60 The late 13th – early 14th c. C.E. translator of the Pāli Jātaka stories into Sinhala, Virasiṁha Pratirāja, notes here four great lakes. Standardly, seven great lakes are enumerated. These are Anotatta, Sīhapapāta, Rathakāra, Kaṇṇamuṇḍa, Kuṇāla, Chaddanta, and Mandākini.

61 The five rivers are the Gaṅgā, Yamunā, Aciravatī, Sarabhū, and Mahī.

62 Regarding Cātummahārājika [The Heaven of the Four Kings], see note 54 above.

63 Paṇḍukambalasīlāsana is Sakka's throne, made out of a red ornamental stone.

64 To seat oneself opposite someone is disrespectful. This is seen to challenge that person's authority. One sits slightly to the side so that the wind does not carry one's body odor to one another, and in such a fashion that it is not difficult to turn one's head in speaking to each other.

these nymphs. He had lost his attraction to Janapadakalyāṇī and he was thinking, "How can I obtain these nymphs?" The omnipresent one said, "If you practice the precepts of your ordination perfectly, you can in the future always see these divine damsels."

On hearing this, Nanda said, "If this is so, I will practice the virtues of my monkhood perfectly. But the Buddha will have to promise me that I will be able to obtain these divine damsels." The Buddha agreed to this.

The Venerable Nanda then decided to practice the precepts of his monkhood perfectly, and he wished to return to Jetavanārāma as soon as possible. From that point on, he began to meditate steadfastly.

After returning to Jetavanārāma, hoping to obtain the divine damsels, Nanda meditated faithfully. The Buddha told the Venerable Sāriputta, "Nanda made me promise that he would obtain divine damsels if he would meditate earnestly." This was just so mentioned to the Venerable Nanda in order to shame him, and to the Venerable Mahā Kassapa, to the Venerable Anuruddha, to the Venerable Ānanda, as well as to all prominent disciples of the 80 great disciples.

The Venerable Sāriputta went to the Venerable Nanda and asked, "Venerable Nanda, is what I heard true that you made the Buddha promise that you would obtain divine damsels if you practiced steadfastly your monkhood, as if you were an employee working under an employer for wages?" In this same way, every time Nanda saw an elderly monk they asked him this same question, shaming him.

Almost all the elderly monks shamed him. Therefore, he felt very much ashamed and he gave up the intention of getting female companionship. And he started to gain insight from his meditation. Developing his insight, he attained Arahant-ship [sainthood]. After the attainment of Arahant-ship, he went to the Buddha and said, "Your Venerable sir, you are free from the promise you gave when we were among the divine beings." The omnipresent one said, "Nanda, as you have attained Arahant-ship, it is for this reason that I am freed from the promise. What I was trying to accomplish, I have done."

On that day, the great elders who were assembled in the preaching hall were discussing the attainment of Arahant-ship by Nanda. They said, "Look how obedient Nanda is! When the Buddha advised him, he followed that advice and obtained Arahant-ship." When they were talking like this, the Buddha came there and asked, "Oh monks, what were you talking about before I came?" The monks told the Buddha about what they were talking. Hearing this, the Buddha said, "Oh monks, not only today has Nanda been obedient. Even in the past he was so." And the Buddha disclosed the past story:

At one time, King Brahmadatta was ruling Benares. At that time, the Enlightenment Being was born as the mahout of a neighboring king who was an enemy of the king of Benares. The Enlightenment Being trained the royal elephant to be capable of fighting in war. This neighboring enemy king at one time decided to fight the king of Benares. He came to Benares with his troops, surrounded the city, and sent a messenger to the king of Benares with a message to fight or give up his country.

The king of Benares heard this and thought, "Why should I give up my kingdom? It would be better to fight." Saying this, he made preparations for war and bolted the entrances to the city. He summoned all his soldiers, and they began to fight.

The trained royal elephant seeing the fighting, with arrows pouring down like rain from the towers of the city, became upset and discouraged, and fled. Then the mahout who was the Enlightenment Being said, "Oh, king of elephants who is renowned to be capable in war, there is no such thing as a war without a rain of arrows. Therefore, it is not appropriate to be discouraged and flee the war." He asked him, "Why do you flee the war? Go forward and break the bolts on the gates and root out the column of Indra at the city gate [Indakhīla].[65] Break down the city's bulwarks, capture the king of Benares, and take him to our king. In this way, win the war!"

On hearing these prudent words, the elephant turned back, ran toward the battle, uprooted the Indakhīla, and broke down all the

65 The Indakhīla is indicative of a king's strength.

watchtowers. He went into the inner city, caught the king of Benares, and brought him to the neighboring enemy king.

Saying this, the Buddha ended the Jātaka story about fighting a war.

"The king of elephants at that time is the Venerable Nanda today. And the mahout was I who am today the fully enlightened one."

The moral: "Obedience to elders leads to prosperity and happiness."

183

The Story about a Flavorless Juice
(*Vālodaka-Jātaka*)

When the omnipresent one who was like a characterizing mark [*tilaka*] to the Sakyā kin was living in Jetavanārāma, this story was delivered about some people who used to eat the leftover food of the followers of the Buddha.

At one time, 500 devout lay people who had left their houses, wealth, possessions including cattle, and so forth, to their own family members became wandering followers of the Buddha. Among them, some attained the stream entrance state of mind [*sotāpanna*-s], some attained the once-returner state of mind [*sakadāgāmin*-s], some attained the non-returner state of mind [*anāgāmin*-s], [and others became saints (*arahant*-s). Out of them, there was not one who did not achieve a higher goal.

At that time, whoever offered the monks food would also bring food for them. There were some voluntary servants who served them, some preparing toothpicks for them, some fetching water for them to drink, and so on. These servants, also numbering 500, used to eat the leftover food of these 500 followers of the Buddha. They were called Vighāsāda-s, as they used to eat this leftover food.[66]

One day those 500 Vighāsāda-s, after going to the place where food was being offered and then eating the leftovers, organized a wrestling game. They were jumping about here and there, shouting out very loudly, and being generally rowdy, creating an uproar. Meanwhile, the 500 devout lay people having retired to their chambers, stayed there being silent.

66 Vighāsāda means, literally, 'one who eats leftover food'.

The omnipresent one, hearing the noise, summoned the Venerable Ānanda and said, "Ānanda, can you please go and see what all that noise is about?" The Venerable Ānanda went to the outside compound and saw that the lads who were the voluntary servants of the 500 devout lay people were running here and there, shouting and playing. He came back to the Buddha and told him what the noise was from. On hearing this, the omnipresent one said to the Venerable Ānanda, "Ānanda, not only today, but even in a previous time while these noble devotees were quiet when they retired to their chambers, these youngsters ran and played boisterously in the compound." Then the Venerable Ānanda invited the omnipresent one to disclose the story of the past. And the Buddha disclosed it thus:

At one time, when the city of Benares was ruled by a king called Brahmadatta, the Enlightenment Being was born as a certain minister who served him.

At that time, in a certain remote state, there was an attack by an enemy king. On hearing this news, King Brahmadatta went with his army and defeated the enemy forces. He then returned to his city, and before retiring, he ordered his ministers to give some grape juice without mixing it with water to the 500 horses as they had engaged in a difficult fight and had won. So, the ministers gave the horses the unmixed juice of freshly squeezed grapes. They asked the king what to do with the large heap of leftover mash from the squeezed grapes, and the king replied, "Give it to the 500 donkeys." The ministers took this left over mash, mixed it with water, and strained it. They then gave the flavorless juice to the donkeys.

The 500 horses that drank the best part of the grape juice stayed silently in their stalls without making any noise. The donkeys that had drunk the tasteless but bitter juice of the second squeezing of the grapes started to run and prance around the palace compound, braying loudly.

The king, seeing this, pointed it out to the minister who was the Enlightenment Being who was sitting near him, saying, "Look, the horses that drank the fresh grape juice, without being overly proud, maintain silence. And the donkeys that drank the bitter and flavorless juice of the second squeezing of the grapes run here and there being overly boisterous. What is the reason for this?"

Then the Enlightenment Being said, "Your lordship, the horses have noble births. Because of this, they are not overly proud and they behave respectably. Menials, on the other hand, become conceited when they obtain whatever they can get. Similarly, these donkeys as they have never before drunk grape juice are beyond themselves with happiness and cannot control their behavior."

The king ordered his servants to strike at the donkeys and chase them out of the palace compound.

The Buddha in this way ended this story about a flavorless juice.

"The donkeys at that time are now these Vighāsāda-s. The 500 horses are now the 500 devout lay people. The king is now Ānanda. And the minister is now I who have become the fully enlightened one."

The moral: "A minor gain should not make a person become conceited."

184

The Story of Giridatta (or, Giridanta)
(*Giridatta-Jātaka, Giridanta-Jātaka*)

While the omnipresent one who was like a lamp to the Sakyā kin was in Veḷuvanārāma, he delivered this story about a monk who spoke against him and who was partial to Devadatta. The present circumstances came in detail in the *Mahilāmukha-Jātaka* [No. 26].

At one time in the city of Benares, there was a king called Sāma [The Calming One].[67] The Enlightenment Being was born at that time to a family of nobles. When he was grown up, he came to serve the king, advising him according to the Dhamma [righteousness] as well as in financial matters.

At that time, there was a royal horse named Pāṇḍava. To train the horse, there was a horse-trainer called Giridatta (or, Giridanta). That horse-trainer was a little bit lame. He would walk in front of the horse holding the rein. The horse thought that the lame trainer was teaching him how to walk, and so he too limped. Thinking so, he walked like a lame horse.

The king heard that the horse was limping. On hearing this news, the king said to the Enlightenment Being, "I heard that the royal horse has become lame. Please examine the horse and see what is the matter."

The Enlightenment Being went to the stable, examined the horse, but did not see any defect. He saw, though, that the horse-trainer was

67 Especially, 'One Who Speaks Calming and Conciliatory Words'. Speaking so is one of the four means of winning over an enemy [*upāya*-s]. The other three are giving well-applied gifts [*dāna*], winning over to one's side by sowing dissention [*bheda*], and as a last resort open assault, fighting in a manner as to completely conquer the enemy [*daṇḍa*]. See, for example, the 'Laws of Manu' (*Mānavadharmaśāstra*) 7.198-200, the 12th c. C.E. book of fables and proverbs *Hitopadeśa* ('Salutary Instruction') 3.7.43-46, or the famous Sanskrit 'Dictionary of Amara[siṁha]' (*Amarakośa*) 2.8.21.

lame. He thought, "As the trainer is lame, the horse is on that account acting as if it, too, is lame." He determined that the horse had no physical defect. He returned to the king and said, "Your worship King Sāma, the horse called Pāṇḍava as a result of imitating the horse-trainer Giridatta who is lame, himself has come to be a lame horse. Therefore, your worship, if you can hire a good horse-trainer without such lameness in his stead, then the horse will have a natural gait." The king did this, and the horse started to walk properly.

Saying this, the enlightened one ended this story of Giridatta.

"The horse-trainer at that time is today the monk Devadatta. The horse Pāṇḍava was the monk who took the side of Devadatta. The king was the Venerable Ānanda. The minister was I who am today the enlightened one."

Saying this, he who was the fully enlightened one ended this story.

The moral: "A bad example will always give a bad result. A good example gives a good result."

185

The Story of Forgetfulness
(*Anabhirati-Jātaka*)

Again, while the omnipresent one who was like a distinguishing mark [*tilaka*] on the forehead for the threefold world[68] was living in Jetavanārāma, this Jātaka story was delivered with regard to a certain Brahmin. This is how it came about.

In the city of Sāvatthi, there was a young Brahmin youth who had learned by heart the three Veda-s. He taught the sacred spells [*mantā*, Sanskrit *mantra*-s] to many nobles' children. Eventually, he married and had a wife, children, servants, slaves, cattle, and many other household cares, and he became involved with the turmoil of lay life. While doing so, he forgot the beginnings, middles, and ends of the sacred spells, he confused them with one another, and he became forgetful.

At this time, one day he decided to go to see the Buddha. In the evening, he took some fragrant flowers, incense, lamps, and other offerings, and went to see the Buddha at Jetavanārāma. When the Buddha saw him, he talked to him, inquired about his well-being, and said to him, "You have been teaching for a long time. Up to now, how many verses have you learned by heart?"

The Brahmin said, "Venerable sir, after my marriage I began to enjoy the gratification of the fivefold sensual desires,[69] and have been occupied with household affairs and the turmoil of lay life. Now, I have forgotten almost all the valuable sacred verses that I knew, and I can hardly even

68 The threefold world is heaven [*sagga*], the human world [*manussaloka*], and hell [*pātāla*]. In Abhidhamma literature [teachings on psychological philosophy], the threefold world is constituted as formation [*saṅkhāra*], alteration [*vikāra*], and characteristic mark [*lakkhaṇa*].

69 For the fivefold sensual desires, see note 25 above.

recall them any longer." On hearing these words, the omnipresent one said, "Brahmin, that has happened to you not only today, but even in the past." The Brahmin said, "Venerable sir, please tell me how it was in the past." Then the Buddha disclosed the story of the past:

At one time, when King Brahmadatta was ruling in Benares, the Enlightenment Being was born as the chief teacher in Benares. While he was teaching a large number of students, there was one Brahmin youth who excelled as the foremost among them. After completing his studies, he married. After marriage, he became involved with the gratification of the fivefold sensual desires and household affairs. Since then, he began to become forgetful of the sacred spells that he had learned. The Enlightenment Being asked him, "Why have you forgotten all your verses?" He answered, "Respectful sir, when I began to become involved with household affairs and the fivefold sensual desires, I became forgetful." Listening to him, the Enlightenment Being said, "Oh young householder, in turbid water, one cannot see clearly shells, fish, turtles, and like things that are in the waters. In the same way, when someone has a mind troubled by domestic problems, he cannot remember clearly what he has learned. In clear water, one can see clearly shells, fish, turtles, and like things that are in the waters. In the same way, a calm mind can remember many things that one has learned with one's mind."

Saying this, the Buddha ended the disclosure of this Jātaka story of forgetfulness.

"The Brahmin youth at that time was the same as in this life. And the foremost teacher in Benares was I who am today the fully enlightened one, the Buddha."

The moral: "Sensual desires and domestic problems cause forgetfulness."

186

The Story of Dadhivāhana [The Curd-Pouring One]

(*Dadhivāhana-Jātaka*)

Once again, this story was delivered by the omnipresent one who was the chief of the threefold world[70] while he was living in Jetavana temple [*vihāra*] on account of a monk who was associated with the Venerable Devadatta.

The present story of this is similar to the previous.[71] Here, the omnipresent one said, "Oh monks, by association with bad people, good people also become bad, just as by the association of a bitter neem tree with a sweet mango tree, the mango tree became spoiled." Then some monks invited him to disclose the past story. And the Buddha disclosed the story:

At one time, a king called Brahmadatta was ruling in the city of Benares. At that time, four Brahmins renounced their lay life, went to the Himalayan Mountains, and ordained themselves as Ṛṣi-s [ascetics]. They built separate hermitages, and lived there practicing meditation.

Then the oldest ascetic died. As a result of his meditation, he was born after his death as the king of deities, Sakka.[72] As he was the king of deities dwelling in the palace belonging to the king of deities, he was able to visit his brothers to see how they were practicing their asceticism. After an initial encounter, he used to come from time to time to visit them.

70 For the threefold world, see note 68 above.

71 The reference is to the *Giridatta-Jātaka* [No. 184]. See the *Mahilāmukha-Jātaka* [No. 26].

72 The position of Sakka, the king of deities, is held by the most virtuous person who has died. A virtuous person is one who practices three desirable qualities, generosity [*dāna*], morality [*sīla*], and meditation [*bhāvanā*].

One day, Sakka came to the eldest hermit and asked, "How are you, revered sir? If you have any needs, please tell me." The hermit said, "I have jaundice. Therefore, I need some fire [to warm me at nighttime]. Please help me get it."

On hearing that, the divine being, Sakka, gave him an axe known as *vāsipharasu*.[73] Giving it to him, he said, "By using this, you can get whatever wood you would like." The hermit said, "Your lordship, Sakka, who will bring me the firewood using this *vāsipharasu*?" Then Sakka said, "Holding this in your hand, ask it to bring firewood already cut up into pieces and to make fire. It will make fire for you itself."

Saying this, he went to the second brother. He asked him, too, what he needed. The second brother said, "Your lordship, Sakka, an elephant path is nearby. Because of this, I am very bothered by elephants. Tell me a way to get out of this difficulty."

Sakka heard this, and gave him a drum. He said, "Take this drum, and if you drum on this side even a fourfold army[74] will run away. If you drum on the other side, then the whole army will befriend you and be helpful."

After giving him this drum, Sakka went to the youngest brother. The youngest brother also said that he needed something. He, too, was suffering with jaundice. He wanted something to cure his disease and help him regain his strength. The divine being, Sakka, gave him a pot of curd and said, "Whenever you tilt the pot, a big river of curd will pour from it." Giving him this, he went away.

In the meantime, a certain boar was wandering in an abandoned village searching for something to eat. Digging in the ground, he found a large gem. When he put it into his mouth, by the power of that gem he went up into the sky and came down on a far-away lonely island. While wandering on this island here and there, he saw a large mango tree. He put the gem down under the tree, and he went to sleep.

73 A *vāsi* is an axe that chips wood. A *pharasu* is an axe that cuts down wood. In a *vāsipharasu*, both blades fit back-to-back in one handle.

74 A traditional Indian army is fourfold, consisting of elephants, cavalry, chariots, and infantry.

At that time, in a certain village a young man was sent away from his home to search for a job by his parents. He went to a certain fort near the seacoast and rented a little boat. Getting into the boat, he started to go by boat to another country. As the boat became wrecked in the middle of the ocean he jumped into the water holding on to a plank of its wood, and he floated. Eventually, he came to the same island where the boar was sleeping. When he got to the island, he saw the sleeping boar and the gem. Seeing them both, silently he went near the boar and stole the gem, thinking that no doubt this gem has a miraculous power. Immediately, when he took the gem, he rose to the top of the mango tree. There, he thought that he should kill the boar and eat him. Thinking so, he took a branch from the tree, and dropped the branch on the sleeping boar. The boar got up, and did not see the gem. He became mad, and began to run here and there searching for the gem. Seeing this, the man who was up in the tree broke out laughing. Hearing this, the boar looked up in the tree and seeing him, he became even madder. He thought that he would bring the man down from up in the tree and kill him. Thinking so, he started to attack the tree with his head so as to bring the man down. When he did so, immediately he died, having smashed his head hard against the tree.

The man understood that the boar was dead. He came down from up in the tree and making a fire, he cooked the boar and he ate. Sitting there, he thought to go to the place from where the gem had come. By the power of the gem, he went toward the Himalayan Mountains. While he was going through the air, he saw the hermitages of the three ascetics.

He descended at the hermitage of the first ascetic, and stayed there for a few days. While he was there, he saw the power of the axe. He thought even if he gives up his gem, he wanted to get this *vāsipharasu*. Thinking so, he explained the power of the gem. The eldest hermit said, "I also would like to be able to fly through the air".[75] Saying so, he gave him the axe and took the gem. The man who had received the magical axe, taking it, went

75 This is a power very much desired by ascetics in India.

a distance and said to it, "Go and smash the head of the ascetic, and bring me back the gem". Then he took the gem, and he hid the axe.

He then came to the second ascetic's hermitage and stayed with him for a few days. While he was there, he saw the power of the drum. He thought he would like to have it by some means. So he explained to the second ascetic the power of the gem. The second ascetic gave him the drum and also took the gem. Then the man, as before, took the magical axe and told it to smash the head of the second ascetic, and bring him back the gem.

Then he again took the gem, hid the axe and the drum, and went on to the third ascetic's hermitage. There, in like fashion, he also then explained the power of the gem, and took the curd-pot. Then he again sent the magical axe to kill the third ascetic and bring him back the gem.

He now had the gem, the magical axe, the drum, and the curd-pot. He then went to Benares.

When he arrived near the city of Benares, he sent a messenger to the king, saying, "Give me the kingdom of Benares. If not, let us fight a war." The king heard this message, and with his fourfold army,[76] he went to capture the sender of the message. The man took the drum, and beat the drumhead that would make everyone befriend him. Then the whole fourfold army came to him, and positioned itself around him so as to protect him. Even seeing this the king, with his royal courage, took a couple of men and rushed toward the man. The man took his curd-pot and turned it top downward. Curd started to flow forth like a river's flood. Then, many people who were still against him were swallowed by the flood of curd. Then he sounded the other side of the drum, and sent still other people fleeing away. Then he took the magical axe and commanded it to go and cut off the king's head, and bring it back. Out of the army that was to fight him, no one was able to bring their weapons to bear against him. Then many people gathered about, and named him King Dadhivāhana [The Curd-Pouring King]. Naming him in this way, they lead him in a

---

76 For the components of a traditional Indian fourfold army, see note 74 above.

respectful fashion with a big procession to the city and consecrated him as the king, making him their ruler. King Dadhivāhana then began to rule the country in a righteous way.

At one time, King Dadhivāhana was taking a bath in a certain river, having spread about him metal nets.[77] While he was bathing, a well ripened mango fruit came floating from Lake Kaṇṇamuṇḍa in the Himalayan Mountains, at which lake deities would eat. The fruit got caught in the metal net. The fisherman who saw this took it, and gave it to the king. The king asked some forest hunters from where the mango had come whether or not the mango was good to eat. They said, "yes". And he ate it, and it was delicious. Having enjoyed its especially delicious taste, he took the seed of the mango and had it planted in the royal garden. Around it, he had many types of fragrant trees planted. Daily it was watered with perfumed water, water mixed with milk, and water scented by sandalwood.[78] Around the tree were hung various types of garlands as decoration. Also, sweet incense was burnt around it. And both curtains and, showing especial respect, high curtains were hung about it. In the same way, many other respects were given the mango tree.

After three years time the mango tree started to give golden colored honey-tasting mango fruit. Its fruit had the taste of bee-honey. The king enjoyed these delicious fruits, and thought they would be good to send as gifts to neighboring friendly kings. But he thought that if the other kings ate this fruit and enjoyed its delicious taste, they might plant its seed, thereby ruining the tree's value. So he devised a stratagem to prevent this. He pricked with a fish bone the seed of each fruit he sent in the place from where the sprout would come, so that it could not sprout.

Those kings who received these gifts of a mango tried to plant the seeds in their gardens, also. But the seeds would not take root and sprout. So they examined the seeds to find the reason for this, and they saw that

77 This was to prevent crocodiles and the like from coming near.

78 Water scented with sandalwood shows especial respect, more so than just plain perfumed water.

these mangoes had been sent with the seeds pricked by a fishbone in the place from where they would sprout.

Knowing this, one king decided to devise a stratagem to ruin the taste of the mangoes. He dispatched a certain gardener, sending him to King Dadhivāhana to carry out this venture. The gardener went to Benares, and announced his arrival to King Dadhivāhana. The king summoned him, and examined him as to whether or not he was a good gardener. He said, "Yes, your lordship. I even know how to make fruit ripen and flowers bloom in the off-season." Hearing this, the king became very happy, and he appointed him to work with his former gardener. And within a few months, he showed the results of his gardening by the unseasonable blooming and fruition of flowers and fruit in the garden.

After seeing these results of the new gardener, the king became very happy. He dismissed his former gardener, and the new gardener was put in his place. The new gardener was then in charge of the garden all by himself.

The new gardener, when the garden was under his management, resolved to make the fruit of the mango tree bitter by planting around the mango tree bitter neems and creepers. When the new neem plants and creepers were grown up, their roots were bound together with those of the mango tree. This resulted in the course of time in making the fruit of the mango tree bitter. As what he had wanted to do was fully done, the gardener fled, returning to his own city.

One day, when the king was in the royal garden, he decided to eat one of the mangoes. When he ate it, it was not as before. He tasted the bad tasting juice on his tongue, and he spit it out. The fruit of the mango tree had grown to have a bitter taste, instead of its former very delicious taste.

At this time, the Enlightenment Being had been born as a minister to that king. The king questioned him as to the reason for this, despite the tree having had such careful treatment. The minister said, "Your lordship, King Dadhivāhana, around this mango tree there are neems and other bitter trees and creepers. That is the reason that its fruit became bitter. Therefore, remove them all, and the fruit will become sweet again." The king ordered his former gardener to remove the neem trees and creepers, to also take out the soil around the tree and to put some sweet soil around it, to plant many types of fragrant trees around it again, to water it again with perfumed water, water mixed with milk, and water scented with sandalwood, and to also pay respects to the tree as before. He reappointed his previous gardener. And the fruit of the mango tree became sweet as before.

The Buddha in this way ended the story of Dadhivāhana.

"The minister at that time was I who have become the fully enlightened one."

The moral: "Choose your friends wisely."

The Story of Four Blunted Things[79]
(*Catumaṭṭa-Jātaka*)

When the omnipresent one who is noble to the threefold world[80] was living in Jetavanārāma, this discourse was delivered about an old monk who was ordained in the evening of his life. One day the two chief disciples, the Venerable Sāriputta and Moggallāna, were engaged in a discussion about questions with regard to Dhamma [religious law] in the presence of the fourfold Buddhist community.[81] [The Venerable Sāriputta and Moggallāna were very knowledgeable, and were very highly regarded by the community.] While they were exchanging their wisdom with one another, there came an old monk who sat down beside them, making a third. Sitting down in this way, he addressed the Venerable Sāriputta. He said, "Venerable Sāriputta, in your discussion, if there is anything I do not know, please tell me. If there is anything you do not know, please ask it of me and I will tell you." The two chief disciples, hearing this, became offended. "This empty man who knows nothing is comparing himself to us." Having been offended, they got up and walked away. As the old monk had spoiled the discussion that had been taking place, the lay people chased him away.

What happened was complained about to the Buddha by the community. Then the Buddha addressed them, saying, "Devout laymen, not only in the present, but even in the past because of this individual when the two chief disciples were conversing, the discussion was

79 Things blunted for four reasons, by birth, color, form, and voice.
80 For the threefold world, see note 68 above.
81 For the fourfold Buddhist community, see note 7 above.

obstructed by this monk." Then the community requested the Buddha to disclose the ancient story as it had happened.

At one time when King Brahmadatta was ruling the kingdom of Benares, the Enlightenment Being was born as a tree-spirit in the Himalayan Mountains.

At that time, there were two golden swans living in a cave on Cittakūṭa Mountain. When these two golden swans were flying about to find food, they were in the habit of resting for a short while on the tree where the Enlightenment Being was living. While they were resting in this way, in the course of time they eventually became very friendly with the great being. The three used to discuss about the present world and the next world [*saṁsāra*].

One day, in the course of time, the Enlightenment Being and the golden swans were talking on the tree. There came a certain old jackal who had only one eye. He sat down under the tree and addressed the swans,[82] "Oh swans, you are perched up on the tree and are talking to each other secret things. Why do you not speak them to me, who am the chief of beasts." Hearing these words of the jackal, the two golden swans flew away to their cave on Cittakūṭa Mountain, having become offended, thinking, "This menial animal is coming to talk to us."

The Enlightenment Being, who was a deity, appeared in the presence of the one-eyed jackal and said, "Hey, jackal. Golden swans speak with golden swans. Deities speak with golden swans, too. You, a jackal, are menial by birth, color, form, and voice. For these four reasons, in these four aspects, you were born in a lower birth than them. Therefore, what type of conversation can you have with golden swans?" Saying this, the deity chased away the jackal who had shown his conceited nature.

And the Buddha, disclosing in this way the story of four blunted things [*Catumaṭṭa-Jātaka*], ended this story.

---

82 He addressed only the swans because he could not see the deity on account of his status, not having a meritorious birth.

"The jackal at that time is today this old monk. The two golden swans are the Venerable Sāriputta and Moggallāna. The tree-spirit was I who have become the enlightened one."

The moral: "Conceit yields negative results."

188

The Story of the Lion-like Jackal
(*Sīhakoṭṭhuka-Jātaka*)

When the Buddha, who was like a distinguishing mark [*tilaka*] on the forehead for the threefold world,[83] was living in Jetananārāma, he delivered this discourse on the Venerable Kokālika.

The Venerable Kokālika saw elderly monks who were studying the *Tipiṭaka* ('The Three Baskets')[84] and he thought, "It would be good if I also were able to recite in good voice the Dhamma [religious teachings]." Thinking so, one day he went to preach. When he sat down at the pulpit, he could not say anything. He started to perspire all over his body, and he got down from the pulpit.

Many monks went to the Buddha and said, "We thought that the Venerable Kokālika knows the Dhamma. But he knows nothing. Intending to preach the Dhamma, he got up on the pulpit. But as he could not say anything, he just got down."[85]

Hearing this, the Buddha said, "In one of his previous lives, in seeking to roar like a lion, he just howled like a jackal." And the Buddha disclosed one of Kokālika's previous lives:

At one time, when King Brahmadatta was ruling in Benares, our great being was born as a lion in the Himalayan Mountains. While he was living there, he mated with a certain she-jackal and they had a cub.

---

83 For the threefold world, see note 68 above.

84 The *Tipiṭaka* is the Theravāda Buddhist canon, consisting of the disciplinary code for monks [*vinaya*], the discourses [*sutta*-s], and the analysis of mind [*abhidhamma*].

85 This is a common theme regarding Kokālika. See also the *Daddara-Jātaka* [No. 172] and the next Jātaka, the *Sīhacamma-Jātaka* [No. 189].

That cub was similar to the lion king in claws, paws, mane, color, and figure. But his voice was similar to his she-jackal mother's howl.

One time, it started to rain. When the rain was over the lions started to play, roaring. The lion cub, hearing the noise, thought, "I also would like to roar like these lions." But he howled like a jackal. On hearing this jackal howl the other lions became silent, thinking, "What is this howling sound?" At that time, the cub of the lion who was the Enlightenment Being by his proper mate heard this sound and asked, "My father, why does this lion, similar to us in color and in every other aspect, have such a different voice? What is the reason for this?"

The lion who was the Enlightenment Being said, "My son, your brother is similar in physical characteristics to me, but he was born to me by a she-jackal." Saying this, he summoned his half-jackal son and said, "Son, while you are staying here, it would be good not to try to roar."

Saying this, the Buddha ended this Jātaka story of *Sīhakoṭṭhuka* [a lion-like jackal].

"The half-jackal son at that time was this monk, the Venerable Kokālika. The lion king's son by his proper mate is at present the Venerable Rāhula [the Buddha Gotama's son]. The lion king was I who have become the enlightened one."

The moral: "It is wise to know when to be silent."

189

The Story of One with a Lion's Skin
(*Sīhacamma-Jātaka*)

When the enlightened one who is the leader of the three worlds[86] was living in Jetavanārāma temple, this Jātaka story was disclosed about the Venerable Kokālika.

[The circumstances of this story are similar to those in the last.]

One day, the Venerable Kokālika saw some old monks who were learning by heart the *Tipiṭaka* ('The Three Baskets').[87] The Venerable Kokālika saw them repeating it again and again. Seeing this, he thought he would also like to teach. One day, he came to the class and sat on the teacher's chair, but he was unable to say anything and he started to perspire. He got down from the pulpit and went away.

Then, many monks went to the Buddha and reported this. They said, "We thought that Kokālika knew the Dhamma [religious teachings]. And now we understand that he knows nothing. He made known publicly that he knows nothing by himself." Then the Buddha said, "Not only today, but even in the past he expressed his ignorance and publicly displayed that he knew nothing." The monks invited the Buddha to disclose that story.

At one time in the past when King Brahmadatta was ruling in Benares, the Enlightenment Being was born in a certain cultivator's family. He lived by ploughing fields.

At that time, a certain merchant used to have a donkey carry about his commodities. He had no proper place to live. Wherever he went, he would spend two or three days there, living there temporarily. When the donkey would be put out to pasture, he put a certain lion's skin over

86 For the three worlds, see note 68 above.
87 For the *Tipiṭaka*, see note 84 above.

the donkey's back. The donkey would eat plants growing in the field, wandering here and there. In this way, he used to graze the donkey. Doing this, he fed his donkey for free.

One day, this merchant came to the village where the Enlightenment Being lived. Following his usual practice, the merchant put out the donkey to graze. While the donkey was grazing, people saw what they thought was a lion in the field. They became very much afraid. They spread the word that a lion had come into the field, and was grazing. Therefore, many people came to see the grazing lion. And they became afraid. So they went back to the village and got more people, and came with weapons and drums to the field. They surrounded the lion, making a big noise so as to make it afraid of them.

Hearing the noise, and seeing the people, the donkey became very afraid of them. It started to cry out with its own usual bray. The people, knowing that he was a fake lion, attacked him, beat him, and cut him into pieces with their weapons. When the merchant came, he saw the cut up pieces of his killed donkey and said, "You, by not keeping quiet, but crying out with a donkey's bray, have gotten yourself killed by these people."

Saying this, the Buddha ended the Jātaka story of *Sīhacamma* [one with a lion's skin].

"The donkey at that time was Kokālika. And the cultivator was I who became the enlightened one."

The moral: "Pretending to be something that you're not, is not always a successful deception."

190

The Story of the Good Present-Day Results of Virtuousness
(*Sīlānisaṁsa-Jātaka*)

When the Buddha, who became the top-gem of the threefold world,[88] was living in Jetavanārāma [perhaps, Veḷuvanārāma], this Jātaka story was delivered on account of a certain devout layman follower.

One devout layman follower of the Buddha was coming to see the Buddha when he was living in Jetavanārāma. On his way, he came to a certain river named Aciravatī. He did not see the ferryman, and thought, "Why do I need a boat to cross over the river? I have my mind full of rapturous thoughts of the Buddha." Thinking so, he went down to the water and he began walking over the water as if he were walking on a slab of rock. When he reached the middle of the river, seeing the water's waves all around him, his rapture decreased a little. At that time, his feet started to sink in the water. He revived his rapture in the Buddha, and going over the water he went on to see the Buddha.

The omnipresent one addressed the devout layman, saying, "Devout layman, did you come safely and with ease?" The layman said, "Yes, Venerable sir, I came with rapturous joy, crossing over the Aciravatī River as if I were walking on a slab of rock."

Hearing these words, the Buddha said, "Dear layman, even in the past devoted people protected themselves with the joy of rapturous thoughts on the Buddha." The devout layman then invited the Buddha to disclose the story of old.

---

88 For the threefold world, see note 68 above.

At one time, when King Brahmadatta was ruling in Benares, a disciple of the Buddha Kassapa[89] who had attained the non-returner state of mind [*anāgāmin*] was going to cross over the ocean by ship. A certain barber was also coming with him on the ship. The barber's wife, handing over the responsibility of the barber to the devoted man, said, "If mishap occurs in the course of the voyage, suffer it together as if you were sharing happiness."[90] Both agreed. They boarded the ship, and sailed for seven days. On the seventh day, the ship was wrecked. They both clung to the same plank, holding it against their stomachs. They floated to a certain island. The barber killed many birds when on the island, ate them, and offered some as well to the devoted layman. Meanwhile, the devout man thought, "There is no help to us in this place except the three gems, the Buddha, the Dhamma [the law], and the Saṅgha [the community of monks]." Thinking on these, he past his time.

At this time, a divine cobra who lived in the ocean changed his body into the form of a ship filled up with seven kinds of wealth.[91] And the ocean deity changed himself into a garlanded ship's conductor. He called out, asking, "Are you going to Benares?" The devout layman said, "Yes, we are going to Benares." The deity who was the garlanded ship's conductor said, "That is good. This ship is here because of you. Get into the ship." The devout man called to the barber to get into the ship. The deity said, "You have permission to come, but he has no such permission." The devout man asked, "Why cannot he get in?" The deity said, "Only those who have taken shelter in the three refuges [that is, the three gems] can board. Others cannot."

The devout man said, "The fruit of whatever virtues I have observed, he also can rejoice in." Then the barber said, "Thank you, sir. I was unable

89 Kassapa is a former Buddha, the one immediately preceding Gotama Buddha. He is said to have predicted the latter.

90 In different words, "Take care of each other."

91 The seven kinds of wealth [*ratana*-s] are gold [*suvaṇṇa*], silver [*rajata*], pearl [*muttā*], crystal [*maṇi*], lapis lazuli [*veḷuriya*], diamond [*vajira*], and coral [*pavāḷa*].

to acquire any merit, but I rejoice in the merit you are giving to me." Saying this, he rejoiced in the merit, thereby purifying his mind. Then the barber was accepted onto the ship. And they started to sail. From the ocean, they came up the river. And by going up the river, they reached Benares. There, the devout man and the barber both got down from the ship and went into Benares. They each went to their own homes. Once home, they found there new wealth created by the deity. The divine being, sitting in the sky, said so as all Benares' citizens could hear, "If someone associates with a virtuous person who pays respect to the three gems, such a person even in the middle of the ocean will get help as a result of that virtue. You can all see that here." He said further, "When virtuous people associate with others, by their power the others also attain good results, just as here one who has no virtue like this barber obtained refuge and wealth."

Saying this, the Buddha ended the Jātaka story of *Sīlānisaṁa* [the good present-day results of virtuousness].

"The devout man at that time attained *nibbāna* [release from rebecoming]. The king cobra is the Venerable Sāriputta today. The deity who helped the devout man was I who have attained Buddhahood."

At the end of this sermon, the devout layman who had come to see the Buddha became one who has attained the once-returner state of mind [*sakadāgāmin*].

The moral: "Virtuousness helps all."

191

The Story of Ruhaka [The Blushing One]

(*Ruhaka-Jātaka*)

The circumstances of the present story come in Book 8 in the *Indriya-Jātaka* [No. 423].

[When the Buddha was living in Jetavanārāma, he told this story about an old householder who had become a monk.

At one time, one old householder thought to become a monk. He went to the Buddha and requested to be ordained. After that, when he went on his alms rounds with the other monks, when invited into people's homes, he was given only a small chair on which to sit because he had been newly ordained. When he was given gruel, he was given the last portion in the pot. When he was given sweets, he was given broken up pieces of the sweets. When rice was being shared, he was given the burnt part of the rice from the bottom of the pot. Sometimes, he could not even get enough food. On such days he would go to his previous home and his former wife, seeing his bowl, would prepare and give him delicious, nourishing food. Then, he started to go to his former wife's home daily on account of the irresistible appeal of the delicious food.

One day this woman thought to test him as to whether he was coming there because he was attached to her, or not. Thinking so, she invited four male guests to eat. While they were sitting in her home, she was cooking sweetcakes behind a curtain. The old monk came at that time on his alms round. She told him from behind the curtain that there was no food. She did this two or three times. The third time, she opened the curtain, came out, and said, "Oh, I misunderstood. This is my children's father who has become ordained." Saying this, she invited him in and gave him food.

After feeding him, she said, "Your reverence, you have become ordained. It is very difficult for women to live alone. These are some suitors who came from remote places to marry me. As you are coming to this place constantly, no one from around here comes here. Therefore, I am planning to go with one of them to a remote village. When you were with me, if I offended you in any way, I beg your pardon. Please, maintain your virtuousness."

When he heard these words, the old monk felt as if they were like an arrow that had pricked his heart. He became very upset, and said, "I cannot live without you. I will give up my three robes[92] and begging bowl. I am going to hand over my robes and bowl to my master who ordained me. Send some layman's clothes to me at such-and-such a place."

He then requested from his teacher to take back his robes. The teacher asked him the reason for this. He said, "I cannot live without my former wife. Therefore, I wish to renounce my ordination." Then his teacher brought him unwillingly to the omnipresent master and informed him of his disciple's intention.]

The Buddha said, "Oh monk, you have been made to feel ashamed by your previous wife before, in the presence of the fourfold community."[93] Then the assembled monks invited the Buddha to relate the old story.

At one time, when King Brahmadatta ruled Benares, the Enlightenment Being was born in the womb of the king's chief queen. After his birth, he grew up, and in the course of time he became the king of the country.

That king had a certain Brahmin advisor [*purohita*] named Ruhaka. The king gave him a well caparisoned horse, and said, "When you come to see me, come mounted on this horse."

---

92 For the three robes of a Buddhist monk, see note 15 above.
93 For the fourfold Buddhist community, see note 7 above.

After that, the minister used to come by horse. Many people appreciated the horse. The happy Brahmin said to his wife, "Oh sweetheart, my horse is very highly appreciated by everyone when I ride it." The woman thought to make fun of him. She said, "My husband, most respectable Brahmin, people appreciate the horse because of his handsome trappings. So, you put his trappings on yourself, and you go prance about as if you were a horse. Then people will praise you." Hearing these words, the Brahmin thought that she was being truthful. Thinking this, he put the horse's ornaments on himself and went out into the street as if he were a horse. Seeing him in the street, all who saw him laughed and said, "Honorable Brahmin, it is very good to see you." The king, on seeing him, said, "Has your bile boiled over? Have you gone mad?"

The Brahmin felt very much ashamed. He thought, "I have been laughed at by many, and looked down on by others." He got angry at his wife and went home to punish her.

His wife, understanding that he was coming home with anger, fled through the back door and took refuge in the king's palace.

After a few days the king said to the Brahmin, "Oh Brahmin, when the string of a bow is broken, it can be mended by a knot. In the same way, you should excuse your Brahmin wife and take her back home."

Then the Brahmin said, "Your lordship, when the string of a bow is broken, a new string can be purchased. As this is so, I will get another wife. I will not take back this one again. As she shamed me in such a harsh way, I no longer want her." Saying this, he took another woman as his wife.

The Buddha in this way ended this story of Ruhaka.

"The former wife at that time is the former wife at this time as well. The Brahmin was this monk who wants to give up his ordination. The king of Benares was I who have become the Buddha."

The moral: "Shaming someone can have unpredictable consequences."

192

The Story of a Lucky Woman and an Unlucky Man [The Question Regarding a Lucky Woman and an Unlucky Man] (*Sirikāḷakaṇṇi-Jātaka, Sirikāḷakaṇṇi-Pañha*)

This story is given in the *Mahā-Ummagga-Jātaka* [No. 546].

At one time, a young man called Piṅguttara from the city of Mithilā went to the famous city of Takkasilā and started his studies with a prominent teacher. As he was very smart, he learned very quickly. So he decided to go home after having shown his skill in reciting all that he had learned.

There was a custom in that teacher's family that if he had a mature daughter, she should be given to marry to the smartest student who had just finished with his education. That teacher had such a daughter who was beautiful and like a divine damsel in form. So the teacher, by tradition, had to give his daughter to this young man.

The teacher said, "My son, according to my family's tradition, I must give you my daughter to marry. You will have to take her with you." Saying this, the teacher arranged a marriage ceremony.

Unfortunately, this young man was very unlucky. He was wholly afflicted with bad luck. But the girl was very highly auspicious and lucky. The young man was not attracted to her on seeing her. But even though he did not like her, as he did not want to disobey his teacher, he agreed. He thought, "It is not good to upset my master's mind."

The father gave his daughter to him in marriage. In the night, the young man lay down on the well-prepared bed. The bride came there and got up into the bed with him. The young man then got down from the bed, and lay down on the ground. The bride then also got down and came near to him. Then, he went again to the bed. The bride also came to the bed again, and he got down from it again since an unlucky person cannot mate with the goddess of good fortune. So the bride lay on the bed, while the unlucky young man slept on the floor. They spent seven days like this. Even though he had no desire for the girl, the young man did not want to upset his teacher. Then, taking with him his bride, he said his farewell to the teacher.

On the way, they exchanged no friendly conversation with one another. With there being no mutual attraction between one another, the couple reached the city of Mithilā. When they reached the city Piṅguttara, the unlucky young man, saw a certain Udumbara, or wood apple tree, covered with fruit. He climbed the tree, and began to eat the ripened fruit without giving any to his bride. The bride, who was very hungry, asked him for some fruit to eat. The young man said, "Do you not have hands and feet? If you are hungry, you also can climb the tree and eat." Saying this, he started to eat more.

As there is no greater pain than hunger, even though the bride was delicate, she also climbed up the tree. She then started to eat fruit so as to satisfy her hunger. The young man, seeing that she had climbed up the tree, quickly got down from it and placed thistles around the tree so that she could not get down. He thought, "I have gotten rid of this unlucky troublemaker." And he went off toward the city. The poor girl could not get down, as there were thistles around the tree. So she stayed up in the tree, there being no way to get down.

In the meantime, the king of the country on that day had gone to his pleasure garden mounted on a caparisoned elephant. Returning to the city from his pleasure garden in the evening, he saw the young woman on the tree and fell in love with her. He sent some attendants to find out whether or not she was married. The young woman said, "Sirs, I was given a husband by my parents. This very same husband, leaving me up in this tree, went away and left me here alone." The attendants repeated this answer to the king. Hearing this news, the king said, "If there are no owners, such treasures belong to the king." And the king ordered his servants to get her down from the tree and place her on his royal elephant. He took her to the palace. There, placing her on top of a pile of gems, he made her his chief queen.

The queen was very much loved by the king and she, too, was in love with him. As she had first been seen on the wood apple tree, she was called Udumbarā-Devī.

Time passed in this way, and one day the king thought to go to his pleasure garden again and had his subjects clear the road. The young man named Piṅguttara, taking a hoe, cleared the road, so appointed by royal order. Before the clearing of the road was finished, the king left the palace in procession. Piṅguttara was clearing the road wearing a cloth tucked up from between his legs. The king passed by on a chariot with Queen Udumbarā before the clearing was finished.

Queen Udumbarā, seeing the man who was clearing the road, recognized him and laughed. She thought, "Such a man could not bear my good fortune, and he became this poor wretch." The king saw this and got angry. He asked, "Why are you laughing?" She said, "Your lordship, this man who is clearing the road is the man to whom I was married. When I climbed the wood apple tree, he made it so that I could not get down, and ran away from me. When I saw him, I felt that such good fortune as I am now experiencing could not be experienced by this unlucky man. Thinking so, I laughed."

The king said, "You are lying. Seeing some other man [a previous lover], you laughed. I am going to kill you." Saying this, he took out his sword from its sheath. The queen became afraid of him, and said, "Your lordship, please ask the wise erudites [whether or not I am telling the truth]?" Then the king asked his chief erudite, Senaka, whether he believed her. Senaka said, "Your lordship, I don't believe it. Who would leave such a beautiful woman and go off alone?" The queen, hearing these words of Senaka, became even more afraid.

Then the king thought, "What does this Senaka know? I will ask the erudite Mahosadha." Thinking this, he questioned Mahosadha with a stanza:

"Erudite Mahosadha, a woman who is so beautiful and so virtuous in character, yet it is heard some man does not desire her. Can you believe that?"

Hearing these words, the erudite Mahosadha said:

"Your lordship, I believe it. If the man has no luck, such an unfortunate man can never possess such a woman as the deity of prosperity. They are as far from each other as the shores of the ocean, and cannot get together as if they were the sky and the earth."

Saying this, he calmed the king's mind.

The king, hearing the great being's words, was satisfied and concluded that there was no wrong. With his mind calmed, the king said, "Erudite, if you were not here at this moment I would have believed this foolish Senaka, and I would have lost this gem of a woman. Because of you, I have been saved my queen." Saying this, he offered the erudite Mahosadha a thousand gold coins.

Then the queen knelt down, paid respect to the king, and said, "Your lordship, my life was spared because of my friend, this erudite. I request as a boon from you that from now on he be looked on as my younger brother." The king said, "Yes, my queen. I will confer upon you the requested boon." "Your lordship, from today on I will not eat any kind of a sweet without my younger brother sharing it as well.[94] From now on, day or night, the main palace door will be open to send sweets to him. Such a boon, I want." "Well, sweetheart, I bestow upon you such a boon." In this way, he conferred such boons upon her.

The moral: "The truly unlucky cannot appreciate good fortune. If one is truly lucky, good fortune will follow."

94 Mahosadha was still very young at this time, and like all children he liked sweets.

193

The Small Story of Paduma [One Who is Named 'Lotus'] (*Culla-Paduma-Jātaka*)

The Buddha who became a light to the three worlds,[95] while he was in Jetavanārāma delivered this Jātaka story with regard to a monk who was infatuated with women. The present story is well explained in the *Ummadantī-Jātaka* [No. 527].

[The infatuated monk, one day, going on his alms round in the city of Sāvatthi, saw a certain beautiful woman who was wearing valuable jewelry made out of gold and silver. Having seen such a woman, he became infatuated with her and could not get her out of his thoughts, as if an arrow that was poisonous had shot him. He started to think about her all the time and he became sick, as if he were a deer that had no water to drink. He became thin and lean, and his veins began popping out under his skin. His skin became sallow. He no longer had an interest in the duties of a Buddhist monk, such as the practice of meditation and the like.

Then the monks who were practicing their monkhood properly and who were his friends, seeing him, said, "Dear brother, formerly you had a pleasant face and a serene countenance. But now you are not like before. What is the reason for this?" Without hiding anything, he said, "My friends, I am no longer interested in practicing my monkhood."

Some monks who were ardent in their practices and who were smart when it came to calming the minds of those who are confused told him, "Oh brother, the Buddha has omnipresent knowledge and five types of eyes.[96] Therefore, the Buddha can heal you. He can release you form this

95 For the three worlds, see note 68 above.
96 The five eyes are the physical eye [*maṁsacakkhu*], divine eye [*dibbacakkhu*],

trouble. The birth of a Buddha is very rare in countless aeons, but luckily we have this in our lifetime. We are lucky to have this. Not only that, but to listen to the Dhamma (the Buddha's teachings) and human birth are also very difficult to come by. Because of these lucky opportunities, we have a chance to end the cycle of birth and death (*saṁsāra*). Leaving behind our relatives, we have become ordained as monks, not allowing our lives to let us be enslaved by defilements. Defilements like lust, and so on, are common with small and ignorant living beings, like earthworms. Defilements are to them wealth. The taste of those defilements, such as form, sound, and the like fivefold desires (*kāma*-s)[97] are short lived like drops of dew that fall from the trees in the morning. But their consequences are deep as the ocean. They will give rise to much lengthy physical pain and mental grief in *saṁsāra*. Dear brother, having been ordained in this glorious dispensation of the Buddha which leads to emancipation, releasing one from all troubles, why do you want to think like that (*i.e.*, lustful thoughts)." In this way, they tried to convince him by many arguments of the disadvantages of the enslavement to lustful thoughts. But they failed to convince him.

As they could not convince him to renew his former practices, they took him to the Buddha who was capable of bringing peace into the minds of the confused. They sat down to the side of the Buddha.

Then the Buddha addressed the monks and asked, "Why do you monks bring this monk against his will?" They said, "Your reverence, this monk is confused at this time and dislikes his monkhood." The Buddha who is known by everyone in the world asked him, "Oh monk, is that true?" The monk answered, "Yes, Venerable sir."] Here, the Buddha mentioned that the omnipresent one, when he was fulfilling his perfections, gave his blood, cutting his shoulder, as he was infatuated with a woman. Then the monks asked him to disclose how it was. As he was so invited, the omnipresent one disclosed the old story:

---

the mental eye [*i.e.*, understanding; *paññācakkhu*], the eye of Buddhahood [*buddhacakkhu*], and omnipresent eye [*samantacakkhu*].

97 For the five sensual desires, see note 25 above.

At one time, King Brahmadatta was ruling the city of Benares. The Enlightenment Being was born in the womb of his chief queen. After nine-and-a-half months' time, a son was born. He was named Prince Paduma.

After that, six princes were born. And these seven brothers grew up under the guidance of their father. They became very attached to their father and worked under him.

One day, the king was looking out over the city through his window and saw the seven brothers were coming to serve him with great prosperity and large retinues. And the king thought, "These seven brothers will take my kingdom by force." Thinking this, he summoned the seven brothers and said, "My children, I doubt you. Therefore, do not stay in this city. Go wherever you like. After my death, come back to the city and take the wealth that belongs to you and that was left to you by me, your father."

Then the seven brothers began to cry on account of their having to leave their father. As they could not go against their father's order, they took their wives by the hand and left with them. After leaving, they went on and on until they reached a certain desert. In the desert, they wandered without having anything to eat or drink. As they had no way to quench their hunger or thirst, the youngest brother's wife was killed, and they shared her flesh and ate. The Enlightenment Being shared with his wife one portion of meat that he got, and saved the other portion. In this way, all the six wives of six brothers were killed and eaten. On the seventh day, it was the turn of the wife of the Enlightenment Being.

Then the Enlightenment Being asked, "Why should we kill her? I will give you all meat to eat for today. Eat this meat, and tomorrow we will kill her." Having said this, in the night, when the six younger brothers were sleeping he took his wife's hand, thinking to save her life, and they fled. On the way, that woman said that she could not walk. So he took her up on his shoulders and carried her. During the entire night, they walked. And in the morning, after the sun's rays had hit their bodies, she became thirsty. She said, "Husband, I want water to drink." He asked her, "From where can we get water in this desert?" As she was pleading with him to give her water to drink, and as he had no way to find water, he cut his right shoulder and gave her the blood to drink. In this way, he quenched her thirst, and she became satisfied. Reaching a certain river at the end of their journey, they drank water and bathed. They settled down in the nearby forest, and made a hermitage. Eating fruit from the trees, they passed time as hermits.

At that time, a certain king was ruling in the vicinity of the upper reaches of that river. That king cut off the hands, legs, and nose of a criminal who had committed treason against the king, instead of killing him. The king had him placed in a small boat and let him float down the river. That victim, because he had been short, was named Kotā ['a short man', in Sinhala]. While he was floating on the river, he was shouting loudly and crying. Eventually, he floated near where the Enlightenment Being and his wife had made their hermitage.

Hearing this noise, the Enlightenment Being came near to the river. He saw this man who was floating down the river and took compassion on him. He rescued him from the river and carried him to his hermitage. He made a cot for him and he placed him on it comfortably. Caring for him, he washed his wounds with a decoction of acrid water, and in this way he healed his wounds.

The wife of the Enlightenment Being asked, "Why did you bring here this disgusting short man?" Censuring the Enlightenment Being, she spat on the ground ten times. And she did nothing for the short man. With her doing nothing for the short man, the Enlightenment Being did everything for his recovery. The Enlightenment Being, without failing to do or provide anything for the short man's recovery, healed him within a few days. After he healed, the Enlightenment Being would go into the forest to fetch fruit for his wife and the short man, leaving them behind alone in the hermitage. He took care of both of them the same way.

In the course of time, the wife became attracted to the short man, and they did wrongly. After time had passed with their behaving in this way, the wife lost all attraction to the Enlightenment Being. She determined to kill the Enlightenment Being. One day, when he came from the forest after collecting fruit, she pretended to be sick and was lying in bed all curled up. She said to the Enlightenment Being, "Dear master, when we were both crossing over the desert's sand, on seeing this hill beside which we are now living, I made a vow that if we came to have a comfortable life in the future, I would sacrifice a worthy offering to the deity who possesses this hill. That deity, appearing to me in a dream during the course of the night, scared me. Because of this, it would be good to perform a sacrifice."

The Enlightenment Being, hearing her words and believing that she was telling the truth, supplied sacrificial offerings and climbed the hill with her. Then the wife said to him, "Master, this deity is not an ordinary deity. He is a great being. Therefore, you first offer flowers and circumambulate three times the offering, and make an invitation to him to accept the offering. Afterwards, we will offer the rice and edibles." The Enlightenment Being, accepting this as she said, first offered the wild flowers and then began to circumambulate the offering three times. In doing so, he came near to a cliff. She, being behind him, when he came to the cliff she pushed him off it as soon as she got a chance.

Luckily, the Enlightenment Being while he was falling down from the top of the cliff was caught by a certain huge wood apple tree covered by vines and creepers, all without thorns. As the girth of the tree's branches was huge, the Enlightenment Being could not climb down from the tree. He remained on the tree and nourished himself by eating wood apples. In the meantime, there came a huge iguana to eat wood apples. Seeing the Enlightenment Being, he was scared and ran away. The second time he came the iguana, recognizing the Enlightenment Being as being the same person who was there before, said, "Why are you up in this tree?" The Enlightenment Being replied to him, telling him what had happened. The iguana comforted him, saying, "Do not be afraid. Hold onto my back." Saying this, he took him down the tree, bringing him to the ground, and went away into the forest.

The Enlightenment Being went down a certain footpath and came to a certain village. There he heard that his father, the king, was dead. He returned to his father's city and claimed the kingdom, becoming the king. He ruled the country very righteously, spending 600 thousand gold coins a day for the purpose of feeding the poor, having made many places in which to distribute the food.

In the meantime, the wife and the short man came out from the hermitage to a remote village, his wife carrying the short man in a basket on her head. There they lived by begging. Many people, seeing the wife, asked her, "Who is this man?" She answered, "He is my loving husband who was given to me in marriage by my aunt and uncle when I was a young girl. Therefore, when he came to suffer like this, how can I give him up? On this account, I am wandering, carrying him like this."

Many people, hearing this, though that she spoke the truth. Thinking so, they gave her and the short man food to eat and other necessities in plenty. Some people, seeing them, said, "Why do you suffer wandering like this? King Mahā Paduma has set up many places to give food to beggars like you. You ought to go to one of those shelters, and you can live there happily." Hearing those words, she decided to go to Benares. There, she proceeded to one of the shelters where food was offered. One day, the Enlightenment Being came to visit one of the shelters offering food to beggars. He distributed food to the poor people with his own hands.[98] After giving to four or five people, he said to his servants, "Give in the same way to the other people as well." Then he mounted his royal elephant and began to return to the palace. In the meantime, the wife carrying the short man in a basket on her head left the shelter after having eaten with the other beggars.

The king saw his wife and the short man, and recognizing them, he summoned them near to him. He requested her to place the short man on the ground. He then asked, "Who are you?" The wife, without any

98 Giving *dāna* [charity] with one's own hands gives one more merit than requesting someone else to do it for you.

hesitation, said, "This is my husband who was given me in marriage by my aunt and uncle."

Hearing these words, the king asked, "Is that true?" She said boldly, "Yes, your lordship." Many people, hearing that answer, appreciated her.

The king said, "I know that your father was such-and-such a king. Your mother was such-and-such a queen. You were a royal princess. I am the Prince Mahā Paduma who cooked food for you and fed you. How is it that you say this short man was given to you as a husband by your aunt and uncle? Why do you think that I had died, and go about wandering with this man on your head?"

Asking these questions, the king addressed his ministers saying, "Oh ministers, did I not tell you in the beginning what had happened? The seven of us brothers came to the desert. Six of the brothers' wives were killed and eaten. I saved this woman while others were eating their wives' flesh, gave her my blood to quench her thirst, and satisfied this woman in every way. The short man whose hands, legs, and nose had been cut off, when he was floating down the river I took him out from it, gave him medical treatment, and protected him in the same way as this woman. This woman, having become infatuated with him, pushed me down a cliff. But I survived the fall, which was broken by a huge wood apple tree. An iguana saved me by taking me down from the tree. This way in which I came back to the kingdom has been told to all of you earlier. That short man is this short man. The Prince Paduma who was pushed off the cliff was I. Therefore, this short man who looks like a corpse ought to be punished by being beaten with clubs. She ought to have her ears and nose cut off. And both of them, after, ought to be cut into pieces." Then, quenching his anger, he said further, "Let her take the short man again in a basket on her head, and tie the basket to her head. Let them leave here, and forever stay outside this city!"

Saying this, the Buddha ended this *Culla-Paduma-Jātaka.*

"The seven brothers at that time are today certain of the monks who are close to the Buddha. The wife was the damsel Ciñcā. The short man was the monk Devadatta. The iguana was the Venerable Ānanda. I, myself, the Buddha was Prince Paduma."

The moral: "It is not good to act out of infatuation."

194

The Story of a Jewel Thief
(*Maṇicora-Jātaka*)

When the omnipresent one who became a distinguishing mark [*tilaka*] on the forehead of the threefold world[99] was living at the temple in the Bamboo Grove [Veḷuvanārāma] there was an attempt made by Devadatta to kill him, which failed. This Jātaka story was delivered with regard to this occurrence. This is how it was.

One day, the monks assembled in the evening in the preaching hall were talking about the attempt made by the monk Devadatta to kill the Buddha, but he could not do any harm to him, not even a minor injury. When the Buddha came there, the monks were talking about this event. The Buddha asked, "Oh monks, what were you talking about before I came here?" And the monks told him what they were talking about. Then the Buddha said, "Oh monks, not only today, but even in the past Devadatta tried to kill me, but he failed to inflict on me even a slight wound." The monks invited the Buddha to disclose the story obscured by time.

At one time, King Brahmadatta was ruling in Benares. The Enlightenment Being was born in a remote village. He married a girl from Benares who was very beautiful and who was endowed with the five beauties [*pañcakalyāṇa*-s] of a woman,[100] who was just like a divine damsel as beautiful as a Kinnara,[101] and who was captivating to everyone who saw

---

99 For the threefold world, see note 68 above.

100 The five beauties of a woman are long hair [*kesakalyāṇa*], shapely form [*maṁsakalyāṇa*], good teeth [*aṭṭhikalyāṇa*], fair complexion [*chavikalyāṇa*], and young age [*vayakalyāṇa*].

101 A Kinnara is a mythical celestial animal with the upper torso of a beautiful woman and the lower part of the body like a bird.

her. She guarded her chastity to all except her husband and was dutiful to her husband's elderly parents, caring for all their needs. Because of all this, her husband loved her very much, and she loved him very much. They lived a very happy life. Her name was Sujātā [One Who is Well Born].

One day this woman, Sujātā, said to her husband, "I would like to go to Benares to see my parents." The Enlightenment Being agreed to this, accepting it. They then prepared the necessary sweets, such as oilcakes, and so forth, which are proper to bring when visiting one's parents. And they set out in a chariot with the Enlightenment Being sitting in the front, driving it. His wife, Sujātā, wearing beautiful garments, sat in the chariot behind him.

In this way, they came to the city and drove through it. At that time the king of Benares, making a circuit around the city on his beautifully caparisoned elephant, passed them on the road. At the time he was passing them, the Enlightenment Being's wife had gotten down from the chariot and was walking behind it as if she were a swan. On seeing her graceful beauty, the king's mind became captivated with her. He summoned a minister and said, "Find out whether that woman who is walking there is married or unmarried."

The minister went to her and asked, "Are you married or not?" She said, "I am married." Knowing this, he went to the king and said, "Your lordship, the driver of the chariot is her husband." Hearing this, the king without ridding his mind of his captivation, thought to get her by some stratagem, even if it meant killing this man. Thinking this, the king summoned another minister and said to him, "Take this precious stone from my crown and place it in the chariot that man is driving." The minister did this, and reported it to the king. Hearing this, the king exclaimed very loudly so all could hear, "I have lost the central jewel from my crown!" The ministers closed all the gates to the city and had watchmen guard all the gates. They began to search throughout the city, and the city was in confusion with people running here and there.

The minister who had put the jewel in the chariot came near to the chariot and said, "I want to search your chariot." And he found the jewel inside the chariot. Taking it out from the chariot, he said, "This is the thief of the gem!" Saying this, he beat the Enlightenment Being, making him weak. He placed his hands behind his back and tied them together. And in this way, he took him to the king. He said, "Your lordship, here is the robber of the gem."

The king, without asking anything, said, "Behead him!" Then the king's officers took him with anger, and ringing thousands of death bells,[102] they carried the Enlightenment Being through the southern gate of the city,[103] and making him lie down on his back looking up at the sky, they got ready to cut off his head.

The Enlightenment Being's wife, who had chased after him, saw this. On seeing the axe that was being brought to execute him, she cried out, "Oh dear master! Because of me you came to such a suffering. What a world this is in which such disasters can come upon people like you who are blameless! If deities protect the world and if there is a Brahma who created this universe, why do they not prevent this type of injustice? As I maintained chastity on your account, is there no reward for that virtuousness?"

Then by the power of the thought of the chaste woman Sujātā,[104] the Paṇḍukambalasilāsana seat of Sakka became hot.[105] Then Sakka looked down on the world with his thousand eyes to see who was trying to

---

102 When there is going to be an execution, bells are rung to summon the citizens of the city to witness it.

103 The place of death is always to the south of the city. One finds here the place of execution and the charnel grounds where bodies are placed for animals to eat them.

104 Chaste women are very much respected in South Asia. Chastity is believed to give them a psychogenic power.

105 Sakka is the king of the gods. His throne is made of a very red ornamental stone [*paṇḍukambala*]. When he sits on his throne, it is so comfortable that he sinks into it up to his navel. When someone who is truly righteous in the human world comes into trouble, his seat becomes hot. Seeing with his thousand eyes, he then examines the reasons for this. And he comes to help that person, releasing him or her from trouble.

take his position by their greater merit.[106] When he investigated, he saw what was happening and he decided to go there and intervene. Secretly, he came there and took the Enlightenment Being who was about to be beheaded, decked him with all sorts of ornaments and rich clothes, and placed him on the elephant on which the king was sitting. And he placed the king on the spot where the Enlightenment Being had been placed to be beheaded. The axe fell on the neck of the king and his head was cut from his body. After this, the people saw that the king of Benares had been killed instead of the Enlightenment Being.

The king of the gods ascended into the sky with his own power, becoming visible to everyone. Many people, such as Brahmins, householders, and so on, saw the god Sakka and rejoiced, thinking, "That unrighteous king has been killed. Now we have been given a righteous king by Sakka."

Appearing in the sky, the god Sakka crowned the Enlightenment Being, making him king, and making Sujātā queen. The god Sakka said, "When wicked kings rule a country, there is no rain in the proper season. Fear of famine will come. Fear of thieves, and the like, will also come. When there are such evil kings, a bad name comes to the country. When they die, they have to suffer in the fourfold hells [*apāya*-s]."[107] Saying this, the god Sakka went back to the divine world. And the Enlightenment Being ruled righteously without causing injury to anyone, and eventually passed away.

---

106 Sakka came to his position because of his virtuousness in the past. When someone who is more virtuous than him dies, that person can take his throne and become king of the gods. See note 72 above.

107 The fourfold hells are the fire burning hell [*niraya*, or *naraka*], the animal world [*tiracchānayoni*], the world of hungry ghosts [*pettivisaya*, or *petanikāya*], and the unhappy birth of a fallen being [*asuranikāya*]. Those who have done severe unwholesome deeds burn in the fire burning hell. The other hells are progressively for people who have done less severe unwholesome deeds. People who die unexpectedly, or with cravings, go to the world of hungry ghosts. In the world of fallen beings, one lives fifteen days in a divine world, and spends fifteen days suffering.

Saying this, the Buddha ended this story of a jewel thief.

"The evil king at that time was Devadatta. Sujātā at that time is now Princess Yasodharā. The young villager who became the king was I who have become the Buddha."

The moral: "Virtue protects people from harm."

195

The Story of the Side of a Hill
(*Pabbatūpatthara-Jātaka*)

While the omnipresent one who is like a sacred receptacle of kindness was living in Jetavanārāma, he disclosed this story about the king of Kosala. This is how it was.

The king of Kosala heard that a certain minister had disregarded all proper sexual restraints in his harem. Hearing this, he went to the harem himself, examined the matter, and understood that it was true. Knowing this, he decided not to punish the minister without asking the Buddha first. Thinking so, he went to see the Buddha and told him what had happened in the harem. He asked whether he should punish the minister. The Buddha said, "Does that minister look out for your welfare, and do you care for the woman?" The king said, "Venerable sir, that minister is a man who does everything for my betterment and who always sides with me. He is one who would partake of poison in my stead.[108] That woman is also dear to me." Then the omnipresent one, hearing these words of the king, said, "Then, when a certain minister is looking out for your welfare, and the woman is also dear to your heart, it would be good to pardon them. Also in the past wise people advised tolerance toward such people as these who had done wrong in the harem, when this had been determined on examination." The king invited the Buddha to disclose the old story. And the Buddha disclosed it:

At one time in the past, King Brahmadatta was ruling in Benares. The Enlightenment Being was the king's advisor with regard to finance and

---

108 In Indian courts there was always a minister who would taste the king's food before the king when there was doubt about it, to ensure that it was not poisoned.

righteousness. One of the ministers of the king of Benares became over familiar in the king's harem. This was heard by the king, who thoroughly examined the matter and determined that it was so. At the same time, he understood that this minister was very helpful to him. The woman also was dear to him. Realizing this, he thought to ask his wise minister what to do and act according to his decision. Thinking so, he summoned his wise minister and asking him to sit on a chair, he said, "I am going to ask you a question. You must solve the problem." The minister said, "Yes, your lordship. I will solve the problem. Ask it of me."

The king said, "If there is a certain lake with the five types of lotuses[109] on the side of a certain hill, and if a certain lion lives there who protects the lake, if some jackal drinks water from it, would it be good to give up using that water, or is it good to use it without setting it aside?"[110]

The Enlightenment Being realized immediately on hearing the question that someone had behaved wrongly in the king's harem and said, "Your lordship, many types of beasts get into a river and drink water. There is no such thing as contamination in such water. In the same way, your lordship, it would not be good to give up your queen. If the minister who has been intimate with the queen is helpful to you, and the queen is dear to you, it would not be good to punish them."

Then the king quenched his anger and forgave the wrongfully acting minister and queen, saying, "If you continue such an association after today, we will know what to do." In this way, he made them fearful of any further association of this nature.

From that point on, they did not behave in such a wrongful way.

Saying this, the omnipresent one ended this story of the side of a hill.

The minister and queen of the king of Kosala never again did such a misdeed after hearing this story of the omnipresent one.

---

109 The five types of lotuses are red, white, blue, yellow, and purple.

110 It is the custom in India not to take water or food that has been contaminated by having been drunk or eaten by a low status person.

"The king at that time was the Venerable Ānanda. And the wise minister," the Buddha said, pointing to himself, "was I who have become the Buddha."

The moral: "Pardoning wrongful behavior is more noble than punishment."

196

The Story of a Horse of the Cloud Species[111]
(*Valāhassa-Jātaka, Valāhaka-Jātaka*)

Once, when the omnipresent one who had a compassionate mind that was like a hidden treasure was living in Jetavanārāma, he delivered this story with regard to a certain monk whose mind was infatuated with a woman. This is how it was.

Once, a certain monk had his mind infatuated with thoughts of a woman. The omnipresent one heard about this monk and he asked him, "Is it true, oh monk, that your mind is infatuated with a woman?" The monk said, "Yes sir." The omnipresent one said, "Oh monk, by being so infatuated, you will fall into the same misfortune as the 500 merchants who came into the midst of blood-drinking female sprites [*yakkhinī*-s]." Asked by him how it was, the omnipresent one disclosed the old story in this way:

In the past, there were many blood-drinking female sprites creating a certain demon-city on the island of Tambapaṇṇi, near the city of Tammanna.[112]

At that time, when men came to the city of Tammanna by ships and small boats, those female sprites lived with them. When some other merchants would come in the same way to the city by ships, immediately

111 Such a horse is born to the world as a result of his good deeds for the use of a Universal Monarch [*cakkavattin*]. He knows the mentality of his master. The Jātaka story here is similar to the early history of Sri Lanka according to 'The Great Chronicle' (*Mahāvaṁsa*). It might be helpful to historians in filling the gap in this history left standing by 'The Great Chronicle' for the period before the Buddha's *parinibbāna*.

112 Sri Lanka was known as Tambapaṇṇi in ancient times. Its capital was called Tammanna.

the former men were beaten and weakened, and then they were put in a prison and were eaten.

If a ship would not come toward the city of Tammanna, from the island of Nāgadīpa to the city of Kalyāṇi, between these two marine areas, they wandered.[113] And if they saw any ship, they would catch the sailors and eat them.

With the she-demons spending their time in this way, a certain ship with 500 merchants sailed to Tambapaṇṇi island.

At that time, the female sprites created for themselves houses and fields that were being ploughed and sown with grain, as well as dogs, peacocks, and many other such animals, and disguised themselves as they desired. The merchants thought that this was a village where there were human beings living, and they disembarked there. When they disembarked, those female sprites came there and gave the merchants sweets and water to eat and drink. And they asked them, "From where did all of you come?" They said, "Our own husbands left here as merchants. And it is now for three years that they have not returned. All of you are merchants, too. Therefore, you can be our husbands."[114] Saying this, those female sprites, showing their womanly natures, persuaded those 500 merchants to be their husbands.

The wife of the chief merchant left him in the middle of the night and, after eating human flesh, came back to her husband and slept. The merchant, when he put his hand on her body, felt it to be cold. He understood why it was so, realizing that she had just eaten human flesh. The next morning, when the 500 merchants and their chief went to wash up, he said to the others, "Hey, these are not humans. These are demons.

113 The island of Nāgadīpa is off the north coast of Sri Lanka. The city of Kalyāṇi is on the southern coast of Sri Lanka. The city of Tammanna is between these on the western coast.

114 In different words, "Our husbands, who were merchants, have been gone for a reasonable enough period of time for us to believe that they are dead. As you are merchants, too, you are of an appropriate community to become our husbands."

They have eaten their previous husbands, after seeing us. If there are newcomers, they will kill us and eat us, just as they have eaten them. Therefore, we must flee quickly."

Then, 250 of them said, "What are you saying? Women like these are like divine damsels! How can we leave them?" The other 250 of them thought, "How can we get rid of them? We must flee." Thinking so, they wandered up and down the sand of the coast.

At this time, the Enlightenment Being had been born in the Himalayan forest as a horse that belonged to the miraculous breed of horses that had the power to go by air [*ājāniyasindhava*], with a black face like a crow, very dark hair like a blue sapphire, and a wide body like a combed lump of cotton wool. Going through the sky, daily he used to come to Tammanna city to graze on wild rice growing in a certain pond. While he was returning home, he would shout, "Is there anyone who would like to go to Jambudīpa?"[115]

When he called like this, those 250 merchants came to him and placing their hands together over their heads in respect, they said, "We would like to go."

Then the Enlightenment Being came down to the ground. Those who could sit on his back, he let them get up on his back. Others held onto his tail. And others, by his power alone, he took them through the sky. And he went to Jambudīpa, bringing them each to their own homes. He then returned to the Himalayan forest.

The omnipresent one said, "Oh monks, whatsoever monk or nun, layman or laywoman, whosoever among these four groups of followers be attracted to women, they will suffer the fivefold punishments. What are these fivefold punishments? They are the cutting off of hands, the cutting off of ears and nose, the cutting off of thumbs, the cutting of the chest, and being beheaded. They will have to suffer these five punishments. Not only that, also they have to suffer the fourfold hells."[116]

---

115 Jambudīpa is an ancient name for India.

116 For the fourfold hells, see note 107 above.

And further, the Buddha said, "Without paying attention to the omnipresent one's words, if one lives with a woman, such a person will suffer like the 250 merchants who became the victims of the *yakkhinī* demon women by not paying attention to the words of the chief merchant. If someone, listening to the omnipresent one's words, corrects his or her thought and becomes no longer attracted to women, by giving up women such people are similar to the 250 merchants who heeded the chief merchant's words and saved their lives. They will enjoy the happiness of the six divine worlds [*devaloka*-s] and the sixteen Brahma worlds."[117]

Saying this, the Buddha gave insight to those who were listening to him. Furthermore, at the end of this Dhamma sermon, he spoke the four noble truths.[118]

At the end of this Jātaka story, the monk whose mind had been confused attained the stream entrance state of mind [*sotāpatti*] the fruit of which was a thousand types of meritorious resulting effects.[119]

"The 250 merchants who paid attention to the chief merchant's words at that time, are today the disciples of the Buddha. And the Buddha was born at that time as the horse who saved the lives of the merchants."

Saying so, the Buddha ended this story of a miraculous horse.

The moral: "Infatuation brings bad results."

117 The six divine worlds are worlds of sensual enjoyment. They are the world of the four great kings [*catummahārājikaloka*, see note 54 above], the world of the thirty-three gods [*tāvatiṁsaloka*], the world of Yama, the ruler of the underworld [*yamaloka*], the world where Enlightenment Beings [*bodhisatta*-s] live [*tusitaloka*], the world of enjoyments created by one's own mental powers [*nimmānaratiloka*], the world of desired enjoyments that others create for you, the divine world where the god of death, Vasavatti Māra, lives [*paranimittavasavattiloka*]. Living beings who have done meditation and have attained mental absorption [*jhāna*] will be born in the Brahma worlds.

118 For the four noble truths, see note 16 above.

119 The stream entrance state of mind is the first mental attainment in one's path toward Nibbāna, or release from rebecoming.

197

The Story of Friend and Foe[120]
(*Mittāmitta-Jātaka*)

When the omnipresent one who was a flood of kindness was living in Jetavanārāma, he delivered this story about a certain master. This is how it was.

Once, a young monk was very confident of his master's attitude toward him. One day, he thought his master would not be upset if he took a piece of cloth. He took it in order to stitch a certain bag for his slippers. Later, he told his master. The master asked, "Why did you take my piece of cloth without asking?" The young monk said, "I thought that you were very well disposed toward me. Thinking so, I took it." The master said, "What friendship is there between you and me?" Saying so, he hit him several times.

This story was spread in the assembly hall among all the monks. Even the omnipresent one heard it. Hearing the story, the Buddha said, "Oh monks, this master even before got angry with this monk for no reason." Then the monks requested the Buddha to disclose the story hidden by time. And the Buddha told the old story:

At one time, there was a king called Brahmadatta ruling Benares. At that time, the Enlightenment Being was born in a Brahmin family in the nearby state of Kāsi. After growing up, he gave up his lay life and retreated into the Himalayan forest. He ordained himself as an ascetic and eventually became the leader of many other ascetics.

At that time there was among his group of ascetics, one ascetic who had adopted an abandoned elephant calf. The Enlightenment Being told

120 Compare the *Indasamānagotta-Jātaka* [No. 161], which is similar.

him the disadvantages of bringing up an elephant. He told him that by bringing up this elephant there would be many difficulties, so he should give up the idea. But because of his fatherly love for the baby elephant he did not give up the idea, and he brought him up to maturity.

When the elephant matured, he became mad with rut. Once, when the ascetic had gone to collect fruit in the forest and did not come back for two or three days, when he returned and the elephant saw him, he cornered him, killed him, and fled away. Then the other ascetics paid their respects to him and cremated him. They told the Enlightenment Being what had happened and asked him, "Your worship, how can we understand when someone is a friend or foe?"

The Enlightenment Being said, "If someone resents someone, when he sees him, he will not talk in a friendly manner with him. If someone does not smile or look at the other person directly in the eyes, he is not happy on seeing him. By these types of behavior, others can understand that someone harbors resentment and anger. These types of behavior are not observed in a friendly person." And he advised the many ascetics to practice the fourfold sublime states of mind [*brahmavihāra*],[121] just as he did. After his death, he was born in the Brahma world.

Saying this, the Buddha ended this story of friend and foe.

"The ascetic who brought up the elephant calf at that time was the disciple of this master. The elephant calf was the master. And the leader of the ascetics who advised him was I who have today become the Buddha."

The moral: "Place your trust wisely."

121 For the four sublime states of mind, see note 26 above.

198

The Story of Rādha[122]

(*Rādha-Jātaka*)

When the omnipresent one who had a river of kindness as his treasure was living in Jetavanārāma, he delivered this Jātaka story with regard to a monk who was infatuated with a woman. This is how it was.

One monk who lived in the temple was infatuated with a woman. The other monks reported this to the Buddha. The Buddha summoned the monk and said, "Oh monk, though you are infatuated with a woman, do you think that you will ever be able to hold on to her? Even in the past, even though watch was placed on a woman, it was impossible to hold on to her." And the other monks asked the Buddha to disclose the old story. The Buddha then disclosed the story of the past:

At one time when King Brahmadatta was ruling in Benares, the Enlightenment Being was born as a parrot. He was named Rādha. He had a younger brother whose name was Poṭṭhapāda. These two young parrots were captured by a hunter and given to a Brahmin to look after.

The Brahmin, who was a businessman, brought up these two young parrots as his own sons. Once, when he was about to leave on a journey, he said to his two young parrot sons, "My sons, if your mother, my wife, does anything wrong, please stop her. Also, look after her happiness, guard against any unhappiness, and share both with her." Saying this, he left.

Once the Brahmin had gone, his wife started to act unrighteously, having liaisons with other men. Daily, countless people came to the home. On seeing this Poṭṭhapāda, the younger brother of the Enlightenment

---

122 Compare Jātaka No. 145, also titled *Rādha-Jātaka*, which is similar.

Being, said to his elder brother, "Oh brother, when our Brahmin father left, he spoke to us and said that we should stop any wrongdoing by his wife. Seeing her behavior, should we not tell her to stop?"

The Enlightenment Being said, "Keep silent."

But Poṭṭhapāda, the younger brother, went to the Brahmin's wife and said, "Oh mother, why are you behaving in such a wrongful way? Please do not engage in such unwholesome behavior anymore."

Hearing these words, the Brahmin's wife said, "Very well, my son. You have given me good advice. From now on, I will no longer do such things." As she was saying this in a loud voice, she approached him in a pleasing way. And she caught him and twisted his neck, killing him. She put him in the fire, roasted him, and ate him.

After a long time, the Brahmin returned home. He asked his son Rādha, "My son, in my absence, did you see any wrongdoing by my wife?" He questioned him in this way. The parrot Rādha said, "Dear father, wise people do not say the faults of others, even if they see them. It is not good to disclose them when the time is not appropriate. By speaking so, Poṭṭhapāda suffered punishment. Such a punishment might come even upon me were I to talk. Because I say this, from now on it is no longer good for me to live here since my mother is now angry with me." Disclosing this secret, the parrot Rādha got the permission of his Brahmin father to return to the forest.

Saying this, the Buddha ended this story of Rādha.

"The parrot Poṭṭhapāda at that time was the Venerable Ānanda. And the parrot Rādha was I who have become the fully enlightened one."

The moral: "Doers of bad deeds will not stop, even though given good advice."

199

The Story of a Householder
(*Gahapati-Jātaka*)

Then again, when the omnipresent one who was the place where compassion dwelt was living in Jetavanārāma, he heard that a certain monk was infatuated with a woman. He summoned that monk and said, "Oh monk, it is not good to be infatuated with women." Saying this, he added, "During one of your previous births, you were also so infatuated. And because of this, you fell into trouble." On hearing this, the omnipresent one was invited to disclose the story. And he disclosed the story of the past. It was like this:

At one time, King Brahmadatta was ruling the kingdom of Benares. At that time, the Enlightenment Being was born as a householder in a remote village.

The headman of that village was infatuated with the Enlightenment Being's wife. Time passed like this. The Enlightenment Being, knowing it, tried to catch the village headman with his wife.

Meanwhile, the time of ploughing came. At the appropriate time, the cultivators sowed their seed. After sowing, there was no longer any rice for eating. So the cultivators were only able to eat whatever they could get. When there were still two months left before the harvest,[123] they went to the village headman and said, "Oh headman, in the course of two months' time, we will be able to reap our harvest. Right now, we have nothing to eat. After two months, we will be able to give you rice. So, give us an ox for us to eat." Saying this, they got an old ox. They killed him and ate.

A few days later, when the Enlightenment Being was away from home, knowing that, the village headman went to his home and dallied

123 The growing season before a harvest is three-and-a-half months.

with his wife. Meanwhile, the Enlightenment Being was coming home. His wife saw that he was coming, but there was no way for the headman to leave. So she devised a certain stratagem. She said to the village headman, "Sit on the ground in the middle of the house and call out to me, 'Give me my rice.' I will go up into the barn[124] and say, 'Of course, we will give you rice. But not yet! We promised to give it to you after two months. There is no rice here. Look at this empty barn.' Please say this to deceive my husband when he comes into the house."

Then the Enlightenment Being came into the house, and he immediately understood what they were about. He thought, "This is a game that they are playing to deceive me." Thinking this, he said, "What is this, oh village headman! You gave us an ox in return for rice we would give you after two months' time. But now, before even a month, you are asking for rice. What rice are you asking for? And this woman, having gone into the barn even though she knows that there is no rice in the barn, of what rice is she speaking? Claiming your position as a village headman, while others are not at home, what do you have to speak about with their wives?" Saying this, he seized him by his hair, hit him as much as he could, and pushed his head into the ground.

After that, the Enlightenment Being took his wife down from the barn holding her by a lock of her hair, and he also beat her and punished her. She was made to be afraid, and was warned not to do such things in the future.

Since that time, the village headman was afraid of even looking at that home. And the woman did not think of doing such things even in secret.

Saying this, the Buddha ended the story of a householder.

"The householder at that time was I who am today the enlightened one."

The moral: "When the cat's away, the mouse will play."

124 In ancient houses, the attic would serve as a barn in which rice and other grains were kept in baskets.

200

The Story of Virtuousness
(*Sādhusīla-Jātaka*)

When the omnipresent one who was like an ocean of compassion was living at Jetavanārāma, he delivered this story about an anonymous Brahmin.

The Brahmin had four daughters. There were four men desirous of marrying them. Of these four, one was handsome, one was old, one was high class, and one was virtuous and righteous. The Brahmin thought, "From among these four, to whom should I give my daughters?" He could not come to a decision. But he was smart enough to know that it had been said that when you select a husband for a young girl, you should seek the advice of a wise person. The Buddha understood this, and he summoned the Brahmin. "Oh Brahmin, you have been in the same situation before." And the Buddha told the old story:

At one time, King Brahmadatta was ruling Benares. At that time the Enlightenment Being was born in a Brahmin family in that city, and he became the city's most popular teacher. At the same time, a certain Brahmin had four daughters. When they were old enough to be given in marriage, there were four men who were desirous of them. Out of these four, one was very handsome, one was old, one was born to a high-class family, and one was virtuous and righteous. The Brahmin could not decide to which of these four men to give his daughters. As he could not decide, he went to the most popular teacher of Benares.

The most popular teacher said to him, "Oh Brahmin, it is good to give a daughter to a handsome man. Also, it is good to give her to a mature man. It is also good to give her to a high-class man. But it is better to give her to a virtuous man than to any other." He said, "Oh Brahmin, if possible give your four daughters to the virtuous man."

Saying this, the Buddha ended this Jātaka story of virtuousness.

"The Brahmin at that time is the Brahmin today. And the popular teacher was I who have become the enlightened one."

At the end of this Dhamma sermon, the Brahmin attained the path of the stream entrance state of mind [*sotāpatti*] that is endowed with a thousand ways of attainment.

The moral: "Virtuousness is respected everywhere."

ABOUT PARIYATTI

Pariyatti is dedicated to providing affordable access to authentic teachings of the Buddha about the Dhamma theory (*pariyatti*) and practice (*paṭipatti*) of Vipassana meditation. A 501(c)(3) non-profit charitable organization since 2002, Pariyatti is sustained by contributions from individuals who appreciate and want to share the incalculable value of the Dhamma teachings. We invite you to visit www.pariyatti.org to learn about our programs, services, and ways to support publishing and other undertakings.

Pariyatti Publishing Imprints

Vipassana Research Publications (focus on Vipassana as taught by S.N. Goenka in the tradition of Sayagyi U Ba Khin)
BPS Pariyatti Editions (selected titles from the Buddhist Publication Society, copublished by Pariyatti)
MPA Pariyatti Editions (selected titles from the Myanmar Pitaka Association, copublished by Pariyatti)
Pariyatti Digital Editions (audio and video titles, including discourses)
Pariyatti Press (classic titles returned to print and inspirational writing by contemporary authors)

Pariyatti enriches the world by

- disseminating the words of the Buddha,
- providing sustenance for the seeker's journey,
- illuminating the meditator's path.

www.ingramcontent.com/pod-product-compliance
Lightning Source LLC
Chambersburg PA
CBHW051821170626
46807CB00003B/967
* 9 7 8 1 6 8 1 7 2 6 6 0 1 *